Without warning he stood and held her arms. The playful expression vanished and he looked into her eyes.

Her gaze brushed over his nose to his full, wide mouth. All she wanted to do was kiss those lips.

His hands slid down her arms and around her body, ever so gently. He lowered his lips to meet hers and after a moment's hesitation captured her mouth. To have what she had imagined turn into reality suited her just fine.

His kiss softly awakened her mouth with a buzz to the senses that didn't require an introduction. While he softly attended to her mouth, she enjoyed the slight twitch of his muscles against her kneading touch. Her enjoyment was like a heady aftereffect from a good wine. She couldn't stop even if she wanted.

"You're beautiful," he remarked. He had to say something to give his body time to stand down.

"Thanks. So keep kissing me."

Books by Michelle Monkou

Kimani Romance

Sweet Surrender
Here and Now
Straight to the Heart
No One But You
Gamble on Love
Only in Paradise
Trail of Kisses
The Millionaire's Ultimate Catch

Kimani Press Arabesque

Open Your Heart
Finders Keepers
Give Love
Making Promises
Island Rendezvous

MICHELLE MONKOU

became a world traveler at the age of three, when she left her birthplace of London, England, and moved to Guyana, South America. She then moved to the United States as a young teen.

Michelle was nominated for the 2003 Emma Award for Favorite New Author, and continues to write romances with complex characters and intricate plots. Visit her Web site, www.michellemonkou.com, for further information or contact her at michellemonkou@comcast.net.

The Millionaire's ULTIMATE Catch

MICHELLE MONKOU

KIMANI™
ROMANCE

Rockville 8—Yvonne, Marjanna, Candy, Lisa, Keely, Christa, Mary—you're the best. Your critique, friendships and hours of laughter keep me on track.

 KIMANI PRESS™

Recycling programs for this product may not exist in your area.

ISBN-13: 978-0-373-86183-5

THE MILLIONAIRE'S ULTIMATE CATCH

Copyright © 2010 by Michelle Monkou

www.kimanipress.com

Printed in U.S.A.

Dear Reader,

Want to know what makes *The Millionaire's Ultimate Catch* special? This book closes my Ladies of Distinction sorority series and launches my new Millionaire series filled with sexy, brooding heroes.

Set against the backdrop of Washington and Haiti, this whirlwind romance captures all the elements of a great romantic story—including a hero with a mysterious past wanting to trust his heart, and a fiery heroine who wears her heart on her sleeve and staunchly goes after her goals, even if they are in the distressingly sensual form of Zack Keathley, a true Kimani Hottie.

I chose Haiti as the hero's birthplace to present the cultural richness of the country and the warm spirit of its people in this romance. Then the earthquake hit, causing devastation to the people and infrastructure there. So a portion of the proceeds from this book will be donated to a Haiti relief effort.

Hope you enjoy,

Michelle Monkou

Chapter 1

Seattle's Key Arena buzzed with the energy similar to an electrical storm. The fans roared their excitement as the women's professional basketball game steamrolled to its final minutes.

Naomi Venable looked up at the oversize electronic game board as a time-out was signaled by the coach. Sweat covered her body. Her heartbeat pounded in her ears. Nothing beat the heady rush of the last two minutes of a close game, especially when her team, the Chicago Ladybugs, led at 88-86. She couldn't help the addiction to this juggernaut to the nervous system even if it was only an exhibition game in post season.

The crowd revved themselves into a cheering war vying for each team. Naomi quickly scanned the seats. Good to see so many young girls enjoying the game. The league's efforts to reach out to them appeared to have had a positive effect. Washington had delivered with a large, boisterous fan base.

The referee's whistle blew. Time-out over. Naomi joined in the huddle chant before reentering the game. Exhibition or not, her effort remained consistent— warrior tactics prevailed. After sizing up her opponents, she decided quickly on whether she had to be a bulldozer and push them aside or if she could put the drills into action and outmaneuver with quick footwork. One way or the other, she was getting to the hoop. A little spilled blood was all part of professional women's basketball, well, according to her rules. She accepted the pass from her teammate and scanned the preset formation for an opening. The six-foot guard slid into position to slow her progress. Naomi grinned. Game on.

Tiny, her rookie teammate, moved into view. Her name was actually Tina, but her small stature had earned her the nickname. Naomi didn't acknowledge her. The final formation to end the game had been determined in the huddle. No one went rogue without a darn good reason. Naomi lowered her shoulders, preparing for a driving rush to the net. Tiny, obviously, had other ideas as she waved madly from her position on the line. Naomi shook her head. She signaled to the other player to shift. What the heck was this rookie doing?

"Looks like you've got a wild one on your hands, Venable," the other team's guard commented.

Naomi grunted her frustration. Off-court many of the women shared friendships, hanging out together with their families. The rookies, however, went through an initiation period where they had to earn the respect of the older teammates. Tiny didn't have a humble bone in her body. She continually tested Naomi, coming up short each time. But her losing record with Naomi didn't seem to slow down her daredevil mentality. Tonight was no exception.

"Why don't you teach her a lesson?" The guard taunted.

Naomi dribbled the ball down court. Seconds had slid off the time with only ten left before the game ended. Two players from the Seattle Storm crowded her, pushing against her body, looking for any weakness to strip the ball. They'd have to wait for a snowy day in hell.

Three-pointer, right here, right now, and she'd shut down the competition with an exclamation point.

Or she could risk passing to the rookie and deal with another risk as Tiny went for the layup.

Her decision took one second. She pumped her arms to take the shot. When the players guarding took the bait and jumped to block her shot, she spun around their bodies. Her shoes squeaked across the floor. Naomi didn't slow her momentum, instead using the power to contort her body to shoot a hard pass to the rookie.

Tiny's eyes widened in surprise, but then the competitive hunger shifted into place with a steely squint and hard line of her mouth. Her small hands clamped around the ball. In a fluid move, she turned, dribbled the ball toward the net and leaped into the air with a powerful burst. All she needed was a superhero cape and nifty outfit to complete the athletic move. She dunked with the flourish of a seasoned veteran, swinging in an unladylike way from the rim before letting go. Her grin spread across her face. Naomi admittedly loved the guts on this young woman. Tiny didn't go for the easy layup. At the beginning of her career, she'd have done the same thing, probably with more in-your-face flourish, yet ending with a technical foul. Tiny represented her past. Her thoughts about her basketball career felt like a final showdown.

The buzzer closed the game. The team had already begun celebrating off to the side. With another shot, Tiny had effectively shut down the game. Naomi hugged her teammates, accepting their congratulations for a great pass.

A win was a win. She caught the bug and joined in the infectious hoopla. Coach wouldn't be happy with the impulsive change-up. No doubt they'd pay for deviating from script. They could all expect a lecture, at a minimum.

Naomi hugged Tiny. She understood the desire to prove her worth to the team. Not too much in life was a solo event. She had had to learn that in the league, with her sorority sisters and was still learning in her personal life. When the opportunity popped up, you followed your gut. She high-fived the rookie. A player had to have that hunger and passion to survive the professionally honed skills of the league. What troubled her lately was that her own love and passion were diminishing.

"Thanks, Naomi. I didn't think you would pass to me."

"You're lucky, I almost didn't." Naomi nudged Tiny, adding a grin to soften her response.

"But then she realized that her old ass couldn't see the hoop to make the three-pointer." The guard from Seattle's team swatted Naomi on the back of her neck.

"Takes one to know one," Naomi quipped. The guard touched on something that she was keenly aware of. The life of a professional player, especially a woman, carried a fast trip to the end. Many players quit the game as they struggled with marriage and children against the brutal schedule and travel. Few returned to have successful careers. Naomi wasn't married and didn't have children, both stages of life she dearly wanted to experience. Would she leave this life to seek the other? In her heart, she didn't want to straddle the two worlds. She headed for the dressing room before they left to repeat this routine in another city.

Naomi showered and dressed in her usual sweats. The others had already left the dressing room to get on the bus. They'd ride through the night and head down to California for the next three exhibition games. She had to admit that going toward the warmer and drier climate would be welcomed, rather than the rainy, cool days in Washington. Sitting for hours on a crowded bus, however, didn't excite her. She treasured her quiet times, even if it meant mindlessly playing with her computer games.

"Do you want me to wait for you?" a teammate called after her.

"No, I'm fine." Naomi waved her teammate on. "Just don't drive off without me," she joked.

She emerged from the dressing-room area and headed toward the exit. One of the arena personnel stopped her for an autograph, which she happily provided.

"Miss Venable, could I get you to meet my brother?"

"Sure."

"He's outside. He's in a wheelchair."

"Did he see the game?"

"Yeah, but my mom took him out early because of the crowd. It would have been a hassle if she'd waited until everyone was leaving."

"I can imagine." Naomi followed the woman, hoping that her brother wasn't too far away. Since none of the other teammates was in sight, she figured that she was the only one waiting to board.

They emerged into the cool October night. The ground shone from a recent downpour. Naomi wrapped her arms around her body to ward off the chill.

"Here he is. This is Ben."

Naomi saw the young boy being pushed toward her by an older version of the uniformed woman standing next to her. She immediately forgot about the cold temperature and hurried toward the child. Despite his small stature, he had a bright, eager disposition.

"Heard you came to the game, Ben. I hope you weren't disappointed." Naomi stooped to talk directly to him.

"It was a lot of fun." He grinned. His excitement to meet her warmed her heart.

"I'd love to give you an autograph. Let me check in my bag, I also may have a towel for you." She dug through the bag. In a side pocket, she found one of the many towels that she normally tossed to waiting fans. "You lucked out. This is all yours."

"Thank you. I like you the best because you visit lots of kids."

"I appreciate that, Ben. My teammates not only visit other children, but many have summer camps for children. I think you'd enjoy yourself at a camp."

"I can't," he said with disappointment. "I have to be in a wheelchair."

"That's not a problem." She pulled out a business card and wrote two phone numbers. "I'll give this to your sister. She can call this number and tell them that you spoke to me. There are really good camps for everyone."

Ben's face lit up with a warm smile. His joy made

Naomi happy to be in his company. She ruffled his hair and wished him good luck.

"Thank you so much. You're awesome," his sister added.

Naomi waved off the compliment. "I love talking to children." She looked at her watch. "Now I must get going. Can I reach the tour bus from here or do I have to go back through the building?"

"You can go through the building or just walk around to your right."

"I'll take the walk. It'll allow me to stretch my legs for a few minutes longer before I have to board that bus."

Naomi shook hands. She took off at a brisk pace, noting how quickly the parking lot had emptied. Although the major streets surrounding the arena carried heavy streams of traffic, it didn't affect the eerie quiet of the parking lot as trees and massive fencing divided the two areas.

As she finally approached a corner of the arena, she had to rethink her strategy. Maybe she should have cut through the building. Although the parking lot was well-lit, there were a few black holes where no lights reached. She was never comfortable with the dark. Even her condo had soft lighting that was on throughout the night.

She broke into a slow jog, wishing for the bus to be right around the corner. No such luck. The parking lot had a few cars, but certainly no buses.

A scream ripped through the silence.

Naomi froze. She looked around, waiting to see if another scream would follow. After a bit, she wondered if she had imagined it. Maybe her imagination was being influenced by the creepy area.

A small number of uniformed personnel emerged from a door, laughing and chatting. They headed for the few cars in the lot. Naomi wanted to approach them, but what could she say? She couldn't even tell from what direction she'd heard the scream and if the person was a man or woman.

Misty rain started to fall, increasing her discomfort. She rounded her shoulders, tilting her head against the annoying onslaught. Her mood soured as dampness seeped into her clothes.

"Help. Stop. Please…"

Imagination or not, Naomi didn't try to figure it out. The pleas eerily served as a call to action. She ran toward the source, not caring that her pursuit took her away from the arena.

She listened for further signs of distress. Naomi wiped the rain from her face in a futile attempt to focus into the darkness. Then she noticed movement.

Large, shadowy figures moved in and out of their circular formation around a smaller figure writhing on the ground. Three to one did not make an equal fight. Now close, Naomi discerned that the victim was a woman.

Memory of being mugged years ago revved her sense of injustice. The savage men who attacked her had never been caught. Suddenly one of the men dropped on his knees and reached out to pin the woman with his thick hands. He turned and nodded at his friends. She used that anger to charge toward the group occupied with their vicious act.

His eyes shifted to Naomi upon her noisy approach. But his discovery did nothing to tame her battle cry as she launched herself onto him. Her shocking entry provided the advantage in knocking him over.

"Run!" Naomi ordered as she and her opponent hit the ground hard and rolled.

The girl, equally startled, stayed motionless for several seconds. Then she rolled over to her knees.

"Get out of here." Naomi squeezed out the request, fighting to detach herself from the brute.

If the girl didn't move faster, she'd have to drag her; she wasn't leaving without her. The girl stood on shaky legs, teetering with arms outstretched for balance. Her clothes hung off her slim frame, evidence of the men's vicious intentions. Naomi hoped she had enough stamina in reserve to keep fighting. They were not out of danger.

A rough hand grabbed Naomi, yanking her head back, pulling her off balance. Pain spread over her entire head. She screamed for as long as she could through the painful tugs. Another burly man stepped before her.

"So you want some too?" His silver lip ring mocked her.

Naomi locked eyes with him. She wanted him to know that he didn't have a willing victim. Her leg kicked out but only connected to his knee. Nonetheless he buckled, but then righted himself. Outrage bristled like fierce static charge from his body.

Whoever had hold of her head released his grip before joining another in his effort to stop the girl from escaping. Naomi cried out when she saw the girl pulled to the ground again.

Now the young girl's cries rang loud and shrill. Her temporary escape seemed to have given her the will to fight. Good.

Naomi turned to help her, hoping that together they could finally escape. But her attacker caught her again; his hand closed around the hood of her jacket. She shot

her elbow into her attacker's stomach. His foul breath
ushered out in a loud whoosh of pain. She hit him a
second time; his grasp on her hood slackened enough
to allow her to squirm free. Freedom seemed to be a
slippery illusion, since she was still only a few feet from
her attackers. Exhaustion flooded her system, battling
against the need to keep the adrenaline pumping in her
limbs.

She ran toward the woman again. They needed a
plan. Sheer desire to escape wasn't enough.

"Don't leave me." The young woman reached out to
her. Her eyes wild with fright.

Naomi's hands balled into fists. Not that she could
take down all these men, but she refused to surrender.

Her fist shot out. The punch landed on the first guy's
cheek with a blunt thud. Needles of pain fired from
her balled-fist up to her wrist. Her hand throbbed. Her
fingers remained curled unable to open. No doubt she'd
sprained her hand. Well, she had another.

A stinging slap across her face stopped any further
musings about her injury. The parking lot shifted around
her view as if someone had twisted the scene on its side.
A new attacker shifted into view. He didn't waste energy
on calling her names. His scowling face and powerful
physique spoke their own language. She tried to reorient,
blinking rapidly to chase away the dizziness. He grabbed
her neck with one hand. His thumb pressed against her
windpipe. The widening smile on his face showed his
clenched teeth.

Naomi grabbed his forearms, scratching, clawing,
hitting. Tears crowded her vision. She tried to open her
mouth, but her brain lagged with its obedience. Right
now, she couldn't breathe. She couldn't hear. Even her
vision wavered like a TV screen on the fritz.

"I'm gonna make you regret meeting me." He peered down into her face. His nose brushed against her skin. His odor turned her stomach. She strained to turn her head. His tongue licked the side of her face.

Naomi barely felt the offense. Her hands fell limply to her side. Her body sagged. She could no longer focus on his ugly features. That must be some kind of blessing.

She closed her eyes. Her grandmother's kind face appeared before her. The older woman was more of a mother than her real mother ever was. Living with her, she'd often heard the caution to stop trying to be a hero. Now look where it had got her. A soft sigh escaped involuntarily from her lips. Blackness covered her as if someone had flicked a light switch to off.

At the end of a long day, Zack Keathley stood in the parking lot of the new retail and residential center. He should feel proud that a new project was near completion. Instead, he was irritated that one of the anchor businesses was threatening to back out of their deal. The economic times had taken the power out of his hands and turned the advantage to his clients. Now the mega supermarket wanted more concessions, trying to tie him up in a deal that would not be to his benefit. He looked at his watch. He'd have to skip dinner again. In half an hour, he had an emergency meeting with his partners to discuss moving ahead or walking away from the table at a loss.

His phone rang. He looked at the screen. *Wil Mem Hosp.* Why the heck was Wilmington Memorial Hospital calling him?

He'd talked to his parents. They were heading off for a weekend getaway. His younger sister was going to a basketball game and then heading out with friends. He punched the button to answer.

"Zack Keathley."

"Sir, I'm the administrator from Wilmington Memorial Hospital."

"Yes."

"This is a call concerning your sister."

"Chantelle?" Zack didn't know if he should have mentioned his sister's name. What if this was some stupid hoax?

"Your sister is here. I'm placing the call on her behalf. The police will be in touch later."

"What's wrong with her?" Zack already moved toward his car. The problems with the retail center had to be set aside for a later time. "I want to talk to her." He waited for the administrator to get his sister. The music playing over the line raised his irritability. His thoughts drifted around creating ever-worsening scenarios for his sister. She was young and in college. He'd warned her about drinking heavily with her friends. Battling with her whenever she came home had become routine. In her eyes, he was the overbearing big brother. And she was his twenty-year-old little sister.

"Zack?"

"Yes, I'm here." He had to concentrate on driving through the neighborhood and toward the highway. "I'm here, Chantelle. Talk to me."

"A group of men attacked me. It was awful. I thought that I wouldn't get away. Could you come for me?" Her soft sob punctuated the teary plea.

"Of course." Zack noted where she'd be. He didn't ask any details because he wouldn't be able to deal with the attack. At least not while he drove fifteen miles above the speed limit.

Twenty minutes later, he turned into the hospital parking lot. He didn't care if he'd parked properly. All he could focus on was getting into the building and finding his sister.

He signed in at the entrance and got directions to the outpatient area.

"Can I help you, sir?" A nurse leaned over the counter at the central station.

"I'm looking for Chantelle Keathley."

The woman looked at her chart. "Oh, she left a message that she'd be visiting Room 316." She pointed farther up the hallway.

"Thank you." Zack walked quickly, peering at the numbers on each room. Some doors were partially opened, allowing limited view of patients and the occasional visitor at the bedside.

A uniformed policeman emerged from a room up ahead. His pace quickened and he entered the room with the bluster of an overwrought brother. His attention lighted on Chantelle huddled in a chair. She sprang up and hugged him.

His arms closed around her. Thank goodness she was okay. His thoughts had turned dark and morbid, despite hearing her voice. He set her down now that his fears had been allayed.

"What happened?"

"I look worse than I am." His sister touched a prominent bruise on her cheek. "It could have been much worse. Luckily, Naomi saved me."

Only then did he take in the complete picture. He stood in a patient's room. A curtain partially drawn shielded his view of the person on the bed. Monitoring equipment beeped their noisy intrusion in the small space.

Chantelle pulled the curtain back completely. He stepped closer, now a bit reticent to intrude. His sister took his hand inviting him closer to the bed.

"Naomi," his sister whispered. "I'd like you to meet my brother."

The woman, heavily bandaged, lying against the pillow, opened her eyes. She blinked as if trying to focus. He didn't know what to say. His eyes drifted to her face and neck, taking in the vivid purple and blue bruises.

"Who did this to you?" Outrage burned in him.

The woman opened her mouth.

"Shh, remember the doctor said that you shouldn't talk." Chantelle touched the woman's arm. "This is Naomi Venable. She saved me."

Zack noted his sister's open admiration. He looked at the injured figure lying in the large hospital bed. Tubes led from her arm up to the IV bags at her side. One hand was encased in a soft cast up to the wrist.

"I heard them tell her that she strained the muscles in her hand. They also bruised her ribs, and she might have a slight concussion. The doctor wants to keep her for observation."

Now, Zack felt his own admiration stir. "Have they caught the guys?" Zack didn't often use his influence around town, but the police chief was only a phone call away. He wanted someone to pay.

"One guy was caught. They're looking for the other three. But also they got evidence from the scene and from us."

Zack's head snapped up. He hated to ask. "Did they—"

"No, neither one of us was raped." Chantelle's eyes

filled with tears. "I'm sorry. I don't know why I'm crying."

Zack pulled her into his arms. Her head rested lightly below his chest. Then he saw the woman looking at him. "Thank you," he mouthed. She slowly blinked her response.

Zack reached down and touched the hand that was free of bandages. He squeezed it slightly, sending his message of thanks again. She returned the gesture. He allowed her hand to rest in his. This woman who'd saved his sister stirred his curiosity but also deep admiration.

"Where did you two meet?"

"We didn't meet." Chantelle smiled at Naomi. "That's the thing. My friend at the game wanted to go hang out at a club afterward. I didn't want to go. I was going to cut through the parking lot to get a taxi."

"Why didn't you call me?"

"I didn't want a lecture," she said plainly.

Zack opened his mouth to launch into one but realized this wasn't the time. He waited for Chantelle to continue.

"First the guys approached like they were all cool and helpful. Then one of them started saying really nasty stuff. I told him that I didn't like it. But they were like a pack of dogs looking for the latest catch." Chantelle's voice hitched. "Me."

Zack rubbed his forehead. He struggled to find the appropriate comforting words when he wanted to declare war.

The woman groaned. He returned his attention to her. Her eyes flickered open. Her mouth moved, but no sound emerged.

"Her teammates found us. Those guys barely escaped. Those women were ready to kill them."

"Who is she?"

"You are so clueless. If you didn't work all the time, you'd know. This is Naomi Venable. She plays for the Chicago Ladybirds."

"Ah." He still didn't have a clue. "That's nice."

"Nice!" Chantelle punched him in the arm. "She played tonight. She risked a lot to help me. Thank goodness the season is over. Could you imagine if this was in the spring?" His sister's eyes rounded in horror. "Now look at her, she won't be able to finish the exhibition games. Hopefully, though, by the time they start practicing, she'll be back to her regular self."

Zack agreed. He didn't need a medical degree to assess Naomi's condition. Bones may need to mend. Muscles needed to be repaired. There had to be some emotional stress from the brutal assault.

"How can I repay her?" Her dark eyes were all he noticed. They didn't slide away from his face but stared back with an intensity that mirrored the woman's will. She intrigued him, stirring a part of him that had so long lain dormant.

"Hello?"

Zack and Chantelle turned toward the doorway. A woman stood there, looking curiously at them. Her brows drew down and suspicion clearly marked her features as she sized them up.

"I'm Zack Keathley and this is my sister, Chantelle." Zack opted to make the first friendly step. "Miss Venable apparently saved my sister."

"Ah." The woman offered her hand. "I'm Wendy Brewster, Naomi's coach. I came to see if she was awake. I wanted to let her know that her grandmother wouldn't be able to get a flight out until tomorrow."

"She's opened her eyes a couple times, but I'm not sure if she's completely aware," Zack offered.

"Her voice hasn't come back yet," Chantelle added.

They stepped back for the coach to enter and approach the bed. Although this was someone Naomi knew, he still didn't want to leave her alone.

"What will happen? I mean, like, will the team have to leave her?" Chantelle asked.

The coach looked up at them; she held back tears with a tight grimace.

Zack tapped Chantelle's shoulder, warning her to drop the matter. The coach would have to think about the team and her obligations. He understood having to make decisions outside of personal preferences.

"Don't worry about me."

Zack was surprised that Naomi spoke, although her voice sounded scratchy and weak. Her face tightened under the strain of talking.

"Always thinking of the other person." Her coach shook her head. "I should be telling *you* not to worry. Your grandmother is trying to get a flight."

Naomi shook her head, which earned a weak groan.

"What's the matter? Should I call the doctor?" Zack asked, concern in his voice.

"Too old…to fly," Naomi's voice croaked.

"Who?" He looked up at the coach for an explanation.

"Your grandparents?" she answered. "I tried to talk them out of it. But you know your grandmother is stubborn."

"Let me take care of getting your grandparents here,"

Zack volunteered. "They can stay with my family." He glanced at Chantelle.

"Oh, Zack, that would be great." Chantelle hugged her brother.

"And when Naomi is discharged, I would love to extend the invitation to her. It's the least we can do for her bravery." Zack wanted to thank this woman, and by offering her his family's home, he hoped to make her understand how much he appreciated what she'd done.

Naomi shook her head. "Home. I'll go home."

"You will, dear, when the time is right." Her coach finally had to dab at her eyes.

A nurse bustled into the room. "Okay, I have to check Miss Venable's vitals. I'll need you all to leave. You can come back in a few minutes."

They left the room and headed down the hall to the waiting area. Zack pulled up short, surprised to see a room filled with very tall women. Obviously, they were Naomi's teammates.

The coach introduced him and Chantelle, which developed into lots of questions about the incident. Chantelle answered as best she could. He learned that the team had to leave shortly to stay on schedule. The decision split the team into two camps, one wanting to stay with Naomi and the other saying that Naomi would want them to continue.

"I know you don't know us, but I promise that we will take care of Naomi and her grandparents for as long as they need us," Chantelle offered. "I'm so grateful to her."

The coach quieted her players. "My assistant will stay here until Naomi is released. If Naomi decides to stay with you, then my assistant will leave and join the team."

"I'm sure she won't refuse. No one can resist Chantelle's nagging." Zack shook the coach's hand. "It's all set. I'll make arrangements." He turned and left the room, not waiting for the coach's response. He had to notify his mother that she'd be having guests for an extended stay at his family home.

He looked forward to getting to know Naomi Venable, his sister's hero. His number-one priority was to show his appreciation for what she'd done. Hopefully she would appreciate the hospitality his family offered. When things calmed down, he could come up with a more personal gift.

Chapter 2

Zack pulled up and parked his car in front of his parents' home on Mercer Island off the Washington coast. He'd teased them over the years about trying to copy British nobility with a stately manor that required serfs to work the large house and acreage. His parents weren't the sort to mimic their neighbors' penchant for showing off their wealth with jewelry or cars. Instead they, especially his mother, felt that, if she built a huge home, then there was no excuse but to have family gatherings there. She also considered it an invitation to have a large third generation of Keathleys. He turned off the engine, also effectively shutting off any thoughts about children and marriage.

Gardeners were hard at work, pruning the trees along the sides of the property. The grass had already been bagged. His mother liked to tend her personal flower gardens surrounding the house, but the bigger job of landscaping was contracted out. The combined effort transformed the house into a gem for home and gardens photographers and the like.

His father had the house built with a contemporary version of the classical Northwest architectural style. The house captured the natural surroundings, making use of the light and space to highlight the best aspects of the changing seasons. With their property set along the Lake Washington shoreline, the home hugged the rugged facing, showcasing its cozy relationship with the natural setting. Zack ran up the brick steps leading up to the imposing double cedar doors.

"Hi, Zack, good to see you." The housekeeper pushed the open door much wider in welcome. "I'll let your mother know that you're here. By the way, Chantelle is resting upstairs. Poor thing, she escaped the attack with a few bruises, but you can tell it still haunts her."

"Thanks, Reba." He brushed his cheek against hers. The older woman had been a stable figure in his life since he was five years old. "Is Chantelle eating?" He worried that she'd suffer post-traumatic stress. After all, the memory of when he first saw her in the hospital easily spurred his bitter thoughts.

"She's not eating much. Had to rely on my bag of tricks from childhood days. Neither one of you could resist my pancakes and maple syrup."

"I do miss those." As he walked farther into the house, the remaining scent of buttermilk pancakes lingered with a teasing trail.

"Then you should try coming home more often," his mother scolded. She entered the kitchen with her arms opened ready for her hug.

"Hi, Mom. Are you heading out?" He noted the

clothes, hairdo and makeup after she released him from a bear hug.

"Just came in. I had to get the guys to pull in a few of the plant pots now that the weather is getting nippy." She headed for the refrigerator. "Do you want something to eat? I do think you've lost weight."

"I'm just tall and the fat doesn't know which direction to move," he teased. His hours in the gym did pay off with a lean, muscular physique. He'd keep quiet about the fact that he forgot to eat sometimes.

"Makes no sense why you're living out there all alone."

"'Cause I'm a grown man, thirty-two." He wiggled his eyebrows. "Kind of kills the conversation with the young ladies if I'm trying to get it on in my parents' home."

"Don't want to hear any sordid details about you and your female friends. The last fiasco with the twins and the hot tub at the country club earned a series of new rules in the newsletter. They might as well have called it Zack's law. Of course, when it's official, I'm the first to know. Okay?" His mother looked over the top of her glasses at him. She didn't release him from her stare until he nodded.

Reba snorted.

"See, even your fiercest supporter doesn't hold out any hope of you settling down. My son, the eternal bachelor."

"Looks like I need to wake up Chantelle. I may need all the advocates I can get." Zack knew he needed to distract his mother from her habitual nagging.

"Don't you dare, Chantelle's resting." His mother poured a glass of lemonade and handed it to him. Then she guided him to the screened-in porch off the backside of the house. "She hasn't talked about what happened a couple of nights ago. Can't say I blame her. What kind of men—" she held up her four fingers "—would do this to a defenseless woman? Our cities are going to…" His mother's declaration turned into a mumble, a habit of hers when she wanted to use a curse word.

"I know. I've talked to the police chief. They are doing everything to find these animals. I suspect that they've done this before and there may be other cases. I told them that I'd bring Chantelle to the station to look at the mug shots."

"You don't sound hopeful."

He didn't respond. The odds were against them, not that he considered the act something unusual among these men. Unfortunately, they would transfer their anger and frustration at not being successful to another victim.

"Chantelle's worried that we'll make her pull out of school in Montreal and enroll in the university here."

"That wouldn't be a bad idea." He could keep an eye on her. As a college student, she teetered on the edge of teenage and adulthood, a position that brought them mutual grief as the grades rolled in. His lectures and advice were rarely appreciated. His impromptu visit to the campus after her recent low grade point average didn't help matters.

"You can't smother her. I'll have to convince your father of that too." His mother sighed.

Suddenly he noticed the increased gray in her hair, which did nothing to detract from its thick, luxurious waves that settled on her shoulders.

His mother stroked his cheek. "It's good to see you, although you look very tired."

"I'm fine." His mother's keen sense of awareness

unsettled him. "Good deals are coming in. Thank goodness things are picking up. There are a few pesky issues that try my patience, but it's all good."

"Nothing more?" she probed. "How are things with your father?"

He shook his head and pointedly looked out at the expansive backyard. The various shades of green fitted against each other like a jigsaw puzzle with flat grassland to clusters of trees. Their house sat on ten acres. His favorite activity used to be exploring and acting out his childhood adventures with his friends. Now he had set aside those childish things for the dollars and cents of his business.

"Your father wants to talk to you," she continued.

"Are you going to be the emissary?"

"Don't take that tone with me."

"Sorry," Zack said automatically.

"No, you're not, but I'll let that go. Will you stay for dinner?"

"I wanted to get back to the hospital."

"Hospital? Oh, right, to see the woman who helped Chantelle. How is she doing?"

"I didn't go yesterday, but I got a report that she's doing much better. Should be released any day now."

"What about her grandparents? I thought they would be here by now."

"Apparently her grandfather is in a wheelchair and needs assistance. Her grandmother had to make sure someone could help him. She'll be flying out tomorrow."

"Wonderful. I'll give her the guest room on this floor." Her mother used the intercom to summon the housekeeper. "What about the young lady…"

"Naomi." He gave his mother the name.

"Will she need a room on the first floor?"

"I'm not sure. Let's wait to see if she's able to walk. Could be painful with the bruised ribs."

"Ouch."

Reba knocked at the door. His mother gave her instructions about the room. From the lengthy comments, Zack knew Naomi's grandmother would enjoy her stay.

"Mom, I have to go," he said after the housekeeper left.

"Why? I thought we could have lunch. I don't often get a chance to have you all to myself."

"I had to reschedule my meeting the other day when I rushed to the hospital. I've got to get this mall deal wrapped up."

"You know your father could help. I don't know why you're being so stubborn. You're just like him." He froze for a second, then forced himself to act normal.

His mother offered her cheek for his farewell peck. "Take care, Azacca. I love you."

"Yes, Mom." Using his formal Haitian name, which meant "spirit guide of farming," carried its own message. She was unhappy with him. He didn't ask for the cause. The list seemed to be growing on a daily basis. His most recent transgression drew the biggest reaction of impatience from her and angry incomprehension from his father. Digging up his past didn't sit well with the family after he gained the courage to share that he wanted to locate and meet his birth mother.

He closed the front door behind him, glad to be on the other side. Out here lay his future, but it also provided him a path to his past. He wanted to know his beginnings. Who was his birth mother? Did she think about him? Did his birth father wonder about him? He hoped his investigation would be successful.

In no way did he not love his adopted parents. Not once did he doubt their love. But he felt that a part of him was missing. Maybe if he'd never known, he could have lived a satisfied life, but the first five years of his life couldn't simply be erased. He had been left at an orphanage in a rural farming community. His name reflected the worker's perception that he was a gift. However, he wondered if he was not just a burden.

Naomi pressed the up arrow on the remote to raise the head of her bed. She didn't want to move, but she had to head for the bathroom. The doctor wanted her to walk around anyway. The torture could take five or ten minutes of sweat and lip-biting pain for the effort. The nurse had admonished her to ask for help. They were so overworked that she didn't want to bother them or she could wait until her assigned nurse was free. Frankly, she was tired of sitting in bed staring at the walls or the mindless TV shows. Her team had gone on with the exhibition, a fact she understood, even if it made her feel abandoned.

Every move she made caused her to bite down. Right now, she needed to hold on to the bed rail and the curtain to maintain her balance. She inched her way to the bathroom, grimacing. Her entire body ached. The painkillers dulled the edge but couldn't eradicate everything.

Her slow walk past the mirror didn't help her mood. She'd asked for two hospital gowns to ensure no embarrassing disclosures. Now that she was in the bathroom, she might as well see if she could wash up. What would have taken a few minutes turned into thirty minutes. Her limbs shook as exhaustion flooded her. A wave of dizziness hit and she sank into a chair just outside the bathroom. She laid her head back against the wall, fighting back the urge to slide off the chair into a puddle on the floor.

"Knock. Knock."

Naomi didn't answer. If it was a doctor, they'd enter anyway. She wasn't expecting anyone else, especially after she'd chased away her coach's assistant. The young woman had hovered at her bedside as though she were keeping a vigil. Thankfully, the woman wouldn't be back until the evening.

"Miss Venable? May I come in?"

Naomi had a good memory for faces and voices. This voice sounded vaguely familiar, but she couldn't place how she knew this. Her eyes barely opened, but a smile spread at the thought that his voice had the quality of a rich, sweet bourbon sauce over a warm, sinful dessert.

"Are you okay?"

Now she had to open her eyes, especially since the stranger touched her shoulder.

"Are you a reporter?" She squinted up at him, fighting to stay focused. "You can remove your hand, now."

"Oh, sorry." The stranger's hand dropped to his side. He stepped back. "I'm Zack Keathley."

Naomi let the name register and then searched her memory. She took in the well-fitted suit, the groomed, clean face, dark eyes that sucked her in with a magnetic appeal.

"Chantelle is my sister. She's the girl you saved."

"Ah." Thank goodness he wasn't a reporter. She desperately wanted to get back under the covers.

"You're looking much better."

"I don't know about that. The mirror just scared

me." She smoothed her hair, now keenly aware that her appearance next to this sleek-outfitted man made her feel drab.

"Glad to see you're up and about, too." He looked at the bed back to the chair.

Naomi slid her bare feet under the chair. Now she obsessed about getting back under the covers. She reached for the hospital gown that was poised to slide off her shoulder. She groaned.

"Looks like you need to get back in bed."

Did he have to look so delicious saying that? Not that she considered herself a flirt, but another time, another place, that would have earned him her sexy smile. Right now, she wanted to cry out from the waves of pain.

"Here, let me help you." He slipped his hand under her arm, careful to avoid the IV tube.

The gown slipped and Naomi tried to wiggle it back into place before she could escalate her embarrassment with a peep show.

"Here, allow me."

"I guess I need to reintroduce myself since you're helping me remain dressed. I'm Naomi."

"Zack." He smiled. "Remember?"

Naomi didn't mind smiling back, grateful that she had washed up. Although her face was a rainbow of colorful bruises, she'd straightened her hair and cleaned her face, and she smelled like soap.

His hands barely brushed her neck as he tied the top. Then he moved to the middle and tied.

"Um…" He paused. "I don't want to go any farther."

"And I don't want you to." She lied. "Now to figure out how I'll get from here to there with some semblance of decency."

He pulled the other gown from the bed and wrapped it around her shoulders. "Now you're all set."

She appreciated his foresight. More comfortable, she eased to the edge of the chair and willed her legs to push her up. She needn't have worried. Zack had his arm firmly around her upper back. They made an odd couple with the IV pole rolling along beside her as he supported her slow efforts to the bed.

She backed her way into the bed. The instant her body touched the linens, she sagged, unable to bring her legs up.

"I promise that I'm not trying to get fresh." Zack lifted her legs and eased them back under the covers.

Sweat sprinkled her brow. She couldn't open her eyes even if she tried. Her mouth trembled. She hoped that she wouldn't bawl, but she'd never felt so helpless.

"Here's some apple juice."

She took the cup he'd just opened and sipped. The cool, sugary beverage gave her a needed boost. She shifted until she got herself in a comfortable position.

"I guess the favor has now been repaid."

"Excuse me?"

"I helped your sister. And you're helping me."

"This is nothing. My family and I are still in your debt." He took the chair she'd just vacated. "That's why I'm here."

"You've been here before, though. I recognized your voice."

"Yes. Do you have any immediate plans for when they release you?"

"No. I haven't really thought about anything. Guess I'll fly back home. I have a long recovery."

"May I extend my family's invitation to stay at our house until you can comfortably travel?"

Naomi didn't know how to respond. Zack, the devilishly handsome stranger, wanted her to come to his home. He didn't look certifiable, although what he suggested certainly belonged in that realm.

"If it makes you feel better, I also extended the invitation to your grandmother. She's arriving tomorrow."

"What?" She'd been out a day or so and her life had been rearranged. "How did you get in touch with my grandmother?"

"Your coach gave me the information. Her assistant has been so helpful with contacting her. Of course, she's upset that she couldn't be here sooner, but arrangements had to be made for your grandfather."

Naomi had wondered about her grandparents. "I was going to call them today…"

"I have her phone number in my cell." Zack, the second time her savior, dialed and then handed her the device. Then he discreetly left the room. Did he have to be so thoughtful?

"Hi, Grandma, it's me." Her grandmother's soft voice made her miss home.

"Hi, sweetheart. I'm glad to hear your voice. How do you feel?"

Naomi gave her some details. Her grandmother called to her granddad, announcing her presence on the call. His distant response made her smile.

"I'll be arriving tomorrow around lunchtime. That wonderful man, Zack, will have a driver pick me up." Her grandmother giggled. "I feel like a star. He'll bring me to you. I can't wait to see you."

"Do you need me to book a hotel?" Naomi didn't want to rely on Zack.

"Oh, no, I'll be staying at Zack's. Isn't that nice? There are nice people all over the world, sweetheart."

"And bad people, too."

"I sense when people are up to no good. I don't get that from Zack."

Naomi pursed her lips. She didn't want to have a futile argument with her grandmother.

"Plus, you'll be staying there with me when you're released tomorrow."

"We don't know that."

"I've talked to the doctor, dear. You'll be released tomorrow. I'll come get you and then we can head over to the Keathleys'."

Wasn't this all nice and tidy? No one bothered to ask her, even though she was under the influence of powerful painkillers. She could expect her grandmother to cave in to a solicitous person, but she was more streetwise. She finished her call with her grandmother, deciding to wait until tomorrow to put her foot down.

"Hi." Zack reentered the room. "Did you have a lovely talk?"

"Don't try to be nice. You railroaded my grandmother into your crazy plan."

"Would you like to talk to my mother?"

"Why?" Naomi didn't like this never-ending stream of strangers all knowing her business. Plus, why couldn't he look uncomfortable, instead of standing there as if he was lord of the manor?

"Hi, Naomi." A young girl poked her head around the door.

"Yes?" she said to the new visitor. Naomi wished they hadn't removed the morphine drip. Now would be a good time to close her eyes and block out everyone.

"Hey, Zack. I was hoping you'd be here."

"You must be Chantelle." Naomi looked at the brother and sister. There was no resemblance.

"Are you getting out today?"

"Tomorrow," Zack answered. Seeing Naomi's surprise, he continued, "Your grandmother told me."

"I wish people would stay out of my business," she grumbled.

"I wish the same thing, too, but Zack likes to play big brother."

Naomi didn't get the big-brother vibe. The man had too much gorgeous material in him to be relegated to sibling status.

"She doesn't want to stay with us," Zack told Chantelle.

Chantelle flopped on the bed. "Really? But you have to stay with us."

"Your brother has helped me already. Debt repaid." Naomi instantly liked the young girl. She had a liveliness that she found contagious.

"My brother always gets what he wants." Chantelle arched an eyebrow, her mouth pursed to add emphasis.

"I have to get to a dinner appointment. Are you able to eat?"

"Yes, although the food sucks." Naomi had barely been able to get more than a few forks of food into her mouth earlier today.

"I'll order you a baked chicken dinner from a friend's restaurant. I'm sure the portions will be too much, but eat what you can."

"Thank you." Naomi couldn't keep up with this guy always sitting in the driver's seat. She'd tell him a thing or two—after she ate the food.

"You know you should just say what's on your mind,"

he interrupted. "Otherwise, I'll have to keep looking at your mouth twitching and those eyes shooting daggers."

"With all your resources, I would like you to recommend a hotel." She refused to budge from her position. She'd never been a burden on anyone and didn't want to start now.

Zack pulled out his cell phone. He stepped out of the room and down the hallway, selecting a spot where he could talk. Normally people wanted to please him, do his bidding, tell him what he wanted to hear. This woman he'd met only two days ago certainly didn't count herself as one of his avid fans and definitely not an admirer.

The phone rang and he spoke briefly to the other party.

Maybe she thought he had ulterior motives for the invitation. He behaved honorably, although his thoughts may have strayed to contemplating things he had no business contemplating. For instance, no significant other had rushed to her side in the past few days. He hoped that she didn't have to hurry back home to anyone. Why did that mole on her neck draw his attention in the worst way?

He stepped back into the room and held out his phone to Naomi. "My mother wants to talk to you."

"What?" Shock was evident on her face.

"I tried to explain to my mother that you were uncomfortable accepting her invitation. She'd like to speak to you." This time he set down the phone on the bedside table and stepped back.

"Oh, you fight dirty, bro. But I like," Chantelle whispered, grinning enough for both of them.

He watched Naomi slowly take the phone. Mothers all over the world seemed to have the effect of making someone sit up straight. In Naomi's case, she tried as best as she could to sit up. Her "yes, ma'am" responses were priceless. Sometimes she began an explanation, but it quickly died. She'd learn that the Keathleys rarely swayed from their position.

"Well, that was unnecessary." Naomi glared at him as she ended the call.

"Have you changed your mind?"

"I didn't have a choice, did I?"

"Then I would declare my actions as necessary." Zack motioned to Chantelle to help readjust the pillows. "I know you've made my sister happy. She looks forward to bonding with you."

Naomi frowned. "You just don't know how much I admire you," Chantelle said.

"It's okay." Naomi looked flustered, but pleased with his sister's attention.

After setting up an informal schedule, Chantelle said her goodbyes and left.

Zack walked to the door and paused. "I want you to relax and recover. You don't have to worry that you'll have to deal with me. I don't live there." What the heck was wrong with him? She didn't need to know about his life. He irritated her and that was very clear.

"Nice to know." She made a face at him.

He smiled as he exited the hospital. He won that round, not that he was keeping score. And what did it matter? She might not stick around long enough to engage him in a battle of wills. He was surprised at his disappointment.

Chapter 3

Naomi didn't care for the car drive or ferry ride to Mercer Island. Her body ached, and exhaustion continued to plague her. The bright spot was having her grandmother at her side. She doubted if Mrs. Keathley could have swayed her decision if her grandmother hadn't already given approval.

Grandma Lucy had practically raised her from seven years old when her mother chose a singing career over motherhood. The wide number of years between her grandmother and her worked to Naomi's advantage because she received the benefits of the older woman's wisdom and life experiences.

"Don't be nervous," her grandmother patted her hand.

"I'm fine," Naomi replied, although she had to consciously unclench her right hand. "Just don't know what we're walking into."

"We're walking into a nice family's home." Her grandmother stared at her before looking out the car window.

Naomi hoped so. From the outside, all the houses looked nice. No doubt the Keathleys were well off to be in this neighborhood with its large, custom-built homes. Right now she had her no-frills condo, since she had no time to dedicate to housekeeping or decoration. She could see herself relaxing in any of these houses when she retired, if she stayed in the league. Hopefully her house wouldn't be for a solitary life.

"You know it killed me not to be with you when I received the news about your injuries."

"The news was slow to get out, too, because coach knew that I didn't want any reporters taking away from the games. I heard that the incident was barely covered in the local news, with warnings issued through door-to-door canvassing. I'm so glad the coach's assistant handled the press. I could never stand there answering to this hero label they've thrown at me. That's a bit much." Naomi snorted.

Her sorority sisters would be out of their minds if they knew that she'd been hurt. She'd eventually call them, but when she didn't sound as if she was talking into a paper bag.

"Oh, my," her grandmother exclaimed as the car turned into a gated driveway. "This home is nothing short of stunning. Wouldn't you agree, dear?"

Naomi nodded for her grandmother's benefit. She didn't want to fall for anything until she was sure that this family didn't have a dark side. Examining her temporary home was cut short when the front door opened and an older woman came out with a cheerful wave. She had no doubt who this was.

"Mrs. Keathley," Naomi offered her hand before introducing herself and her grandmother.

"Please, both of you, call me Frannie."

Chantelle, sporting sunglasses, ran out in shorts and a sweater despite the cool temperature. With bangs and two thick pony tails, she completed the look of a carefree young adult. In giddy fashion, she threw herself at Naomi, who cringed to protect her wounds. "Sorry, I keep doing that, don't I?" She picked up their luggage and headed into the house before Naomi had a chance to make the introductions with her grandmother.

"That child loses her manners as she gets older," Frannie declared.

"You're right. Even my granddaughter here needs reminding sometimes. At thirty years old, mind you."

Enough with having her personal quirks on display. "Um...I'm feeling faint," Naomi lied.

"Sorry, dear. Let's get you inside with your feet up. Reba, our housekeeper, can't wait to fuss over you. Normally Chantelle is off at college and Zack is barely here."

So Zack wasn't lying, he didn't live there. She'd hoped that now that she was a bit more coherent and mobile, she'd get a chance to talk to him. That's all she really wanted, was to chat. Maybe see his smile. Or look at those probing eyes.

"I think we should have a family dinner, so everyone can come together and count their blessings." Frannie led the way into the foyer.

Naomi tried to crane her neck to see the height of the enormous ceiling. Natural light had an open invitation with large windows and a cathedral ceiling. The wood floor gleamed throughout the house. Mrs. Keathley kept a neat and lovely house.

"We have a guest bedroom on the first floor for you, Lucy." Frannie gestured down the hall, waiting for them to follow.

The suite featured a phenomenal view of Lake Washington. Soft lilac tones added a nice warm touch. French doors opened onto a private deck.

"Frannie, this is too much for me," Lucy exclaimed. "I'm a simple woman."

"It's the least I could do." Frannie turned to Naomi. "While your grandmother gets settled, let me show you to your room."

Naomi looked forward to walking with Frannie. She had so many questions and didn't need to hear her grandmother's admonishments about her curiosity.

"Are you able to handle the stairs?"

"Oh, yes, I may have to take it slow, but I welcome the chance to work my legs." As they approached the long staircase, Naomi wondered if she could really handle the ascent. She bit down on the pain and followed Frannie.

"Naomi, I hope you enjoy your stay with us this week."

"I'll only be here for a day or two. Grandma needs to get back home and I'll leave with her."

"Oh, I'm disappointed. Zack said you'd be here for the week. Well, it means that I have to plan the little party sooner than later."

Naomi raised her eyebrows. "Party?"

"I wanted my friends to meet you. I'm so honored to have you, and again, to thank you for helping my daughter." Gratitude shone in Frannie's eyes.

Naomi would have argued more if she could catch her breath faster. Neither Zack nor Chantelle had mentioned any social gathering. She wanted to relax and rest in her room, not be put on display, even with the best of intentions.

"Here we are." They had reached the end of the hallway. Frannie opened the bedroom door. The room wasn't as expansive as her grandmother's but was as tastefully decorated in periwinkle blue.

A feeling of peacefulness overcame her as she walked farther into the room. Maybe it was the color or the view of the garden below, but she felt as if she'd stepped into an oasis. A place of refuge to take her away temporarily from her regular life. She sighed deeply. She had been a bit afraid to allow herself time to slow down. Coming to rest inevitably brought her to think about her future and what she wanted from life.

"Would you like something to eat?"

Naomi shook her head. "No, thank you."

"Okay. Dinner will be around six. Come down whenever you're ready." Frannie left the room.

Her suitcases were already placed in the room. She ignored them and instead eased back onto the bed. The firm mattress felt so good against her tired body.

A knock interrupted her attempt to relax. She bade entry, as she struggled to sit up.

"It's me," Chantelle announced as she bounced into the room. "Making sure you're comfortable." She pulled off her sunglasses.

Naomi cringed. She was used to seeing the bruises on her own face, but to look at Chantelle's brought that night to life.

"You think I look gruesome, right?" The girl touched the area under her eye. "I tried makeup, but I couldn't quite get it right. Then I went to the mall to see if one of those makeup artists could do the job. The woman acted as if I was an abused wife, trying to hide my injuries—no matter how much I explained what happened. I got a lecture."

"I wonder how many women do come through there with those wishes, though." Despite Naomi having many dating failures, none of the men had ever laid a hand on her.

"So then I bought the sunglasses. This type I call the bug eyes because they are so big and kind of wrap around the sides."

"They're cute on you."

"You think so?" She primped a bit. "Cool. When I go back to school, my friends are going to die for a pair."

Naomi relaxed and got more comfortable on the bed.

"Oh, you don't go to school nearby?"

"No. I only came home for the weekend to see my boyfriend. Well, he's not really my boyfriend because he's creeping around with some other chick. I came home to confront him, but then my girls here wanted to go to the game and stuff."

"Has your boyfriend visited you?"

"No. Bastard. Whatever. I threw his crap in the trash. I'm heading back to school by the end of the week…I hope. If it's up to Zack, I'd never leave home again. He's such a pain. The older he gets, the more old-fashioned he gets." She sat next to Naomi with a pout in place.

"I'm sure he's freaked out about what happened," Naomi said with sympathy.

"I guess. He's been acting weird lately."

"In what way?"

Chantelle stopped her musings and looked at Naomi. Her expression closed. "Never mind. I'll let you rest. Mom told me you were resting, but I couldn't wait to see you."

Naomi took the change of subject without pushing back. Her promise to not get involved might be difficult. After Chantelle left, she returned to trying to sleep. This time, she slid under the sheets.

Her thoughts turned to Zack, but only because her plan to leave in two days didn't allow for a lot of time to get to know him. Of course she also wanted to help Chantelle with sound advice and tips on how to deal with her bossy brother. With thoughts of outmaneuvering Zack forming, she closed her eyes and welcomed drowsiness.

Zack sat behind his desk and waited for his business partner to arrive. He could have settled his misgivings over a game of golf, but he didn't want his latest irritation to be underestimated. He wanted Jamison to understand what lay ahead if he continued with his talk about wresting majority control over their project.

"Sir, Mr. Jamison is here to see you." His secretary stepped aside to allow his visitor.

"Thank you. No interruptions, please."

His secretary barely nodded.

"Have a seat, Jamison," Zack said to his partner.

"What can I do for you?"

"I want to know why you're jerking me around," Zack said, his anger barely concealed. "I thought we had a deal with the strip mall in Magnolia. Yet I'm talking to your lawyers instead of you. I'm waiting for you to step up with your financing. Let me remind you that there's still the issue with the anchor store trying to back out of the retail-center project."

"No need to get stressed over the retail center. That'll take a few drinks at the country club. I'm still interested in Magnolia."

Zack waited. His gut issued a warning to go cautiously with this man.

"I want equal partnership," Jamison finally said. "50-50."

"Not happening." Zack didn't need to consider the idea.

"Have you forgotten your promise to the city council? You would invest back into the city by providing ownership to qualified residents."

"Percentage of ownership doesn't equate to 50-50." Zack spoke slowly so Jamison could get the message.

Naomi sipped tea as she stood and watched the sun set along the waterline. Gold swept the sky like a giant paintbrush with flecks of vibrant orange and flaming red. From the house, she heard everyone preparing to sit for dinner. She had to admit to being a bit disappointed that Zack had delivered her to his family and then vanished. In the short time, his take-charge attitude had made a memorable impact. She also couldn't deny the giddy feeling when she was in his company. The man had a way of stirring her thoughts from innocent to scandalous within seconds of his company.

Without him bustling through her defenses, she'd resorted to taking her quiet moments to admire the scenery. She opened her journal to jot down her thoughts of the spectacular sight. Maybe tomorrow she could get a chance to see the full splendor with a walk through the neighborhood.

"You look comfortable." A familiar deep voice inserted in her musings.

Naomi jumped. Or maybe it was her pulse. She didn't want to giggle like a schoolgirl.

Zack stood next to her. "I used to sit out here and dream big."

"The scenery has a similar effect on me," Naomi confessed.

"And what are your dreams?" His voice softened as if to make its owner more charming.

She smiled. "I think I'll keep them to myself."

"I'll share one of mine, if you share one of yours."

"Somehow I think that I'll come out on the short end when I'm not up to my game," she teased. At least he got her humor with a small, responding smile.

He looked back to the horizon. "When I was a teen, I wanted to be a land developer like my father."

"And you worked for him?"

"Through college, and for three years after I graduated. Then I went off on my own. Wanted to make my own name."

"Wow! That takes some guts." She was impressed. "I'm sure it had to be rough."

"Still is, but I wouldn't change a thing."

"I know that feeling."

He looked down at her. She swore that he'd moved closer, or maybe she'd leaned in. The man was nothing more than a human magnet that pulled emotional responses straight to the surface with a white-hot intensity.

From this vantage point, she had a close view of his profile. His features were model-perfect, but the tiny deviations that she had to squint to see added a handsome charm that underscored his manliness.

He suddenly turned, catching her staring at him. This time she was sure that he'd closed the gap. She was proved right when he raised her chin with his finger.

"What dreams did you have?" he coaxed, his whisper like a velvet touch along the skin.

"I wanted to be a basketball player who people would know."

"You got your wish."

"Not really. You didn't know me." Why was she flirting with this man? She couldn't help herself, that's why.

"That's why it makes getting to know you something special." His head tilted down. His lips hovered dangerously over hers.

Now she had another dream, one that didn't require her to be asleep. Her mind meandered with the possibility of those lips touching hers. Given their similar height, she didn't have to tiptoe. All she had to do was close the distance of a whispered breath.

Obviously he shared the same mind-set as his arms gently wrapped around her like a protective cocoon. Or maybe she was imprisoned as his willing captive.

"Er…Naomi, Zack, dinner is ready. Everyone's waiting."

Naomi froze. A heavy mix of panic and guilt washed over her. She kept her gaze locked on the top button of Zack's shirt, dreading to see the housekeeper's disapproval to go with her tone. Nor did she want to witness Zack's amusement at her expense. Not only had her grandmother raised her better than that, her grandmother was in the house.

"We'll be right there, Reba." Zack released her from his embrace.

Naomi welcomed the confident statement, especially since Reba took the hint and left. Her cheeks were still warm, and she was pleased to have a few seconds to regain her equilibrium.

"Not so fast. We have unfinished business." Zack faced off with her, nose to nose.

"Not in this lifetime."

"Want to make a bet?"

"Not a gambler." Naomi backed away.

She didn't get far before he joined her as she made her way to the dining room. She hoped that she'd regained her composure. Having him stand next to her didn't help.

"Oh, good, Reba found both of you. We're starving." Zack's mother waved them into the room.

"Sorry. I was admiring the garden." Naomi felt compelled to provide a reason. She noted that Zack said nothing.

"I am proud of my herb garden. I'll show it to you tomorrow."

"Everything okay? You look flushed. I hope you're not overdoing it?" her grandmother asked. Her gaze pierced through Naomi's attempted cover-up.

"I'm fine."

Zack placed the back of his hand on her forehead quite unexpectedly. A heat flash surged. His touch couldn't possibly create such a strong reaction, could it?

"I said that I'm fine," she managed through clenched teeth, heading for a seat that would put her as far away from him as possible. As long as she was several feet away from him, she'd be coherent and calm.

Instead, he sat across from her. The empty seat near his mother just happened to be across from her chair. Sitting next to him, possibly brushing against his arm as they dined wasn't the problem. Now she had to look into those dark, mysterious eyes that had the ability to be a curtain to his emotions except when he chose to play with her like a cat with a small furry mouse.

"Let's say Grace." Zack's mother led the prayer over the meal. Then the meal began.

"This is delicious," Naomi couldn't help exclaiming. She had seen the perfectly baked chicken centered on the table and the numerous side dishes that rivaled any TV chef's displays.

"I'm going to watch Reba cook before I head home," her grandmother complimented.

"Reba is a natural talent," Zack added. "I told her that she needs to capitalize on this. She can be the next Rachel Ray or that other one that shouts at you."

"Zack, I told you that I'm not interested." Reba entered the dining room equipped with another dish between her hands. She rested the beautifully crafted bowl on the table. "I cooked up a batch of your favorite gravy for the mashed potatoes."

"Once again, she spoils him," Frannie said with a smile.

"Whatever it takes to get him to visit," his father, Paul, said. Silence fell immediately; the simple statement weighed heavily in the room. Maybe the way Zack's face tightened spoke more to the tension.

"I have no complaints." His wife stared at him, her wish plain on her face that her husband cease and desist.

Paul Keathley owned the title of patriarch of his family. He sat at the head and presided over the table in an easy manner. Naomi rarely saw him in the house. He seemed to be constantly working or leaving early before she awoke or returning after she'd settled in for the night.

In the short time she'd known Zack, he seemed to

have taken that trait to heart. She continued with her observation of the two men, hoping that neither would pick up on her interest. Zack matched his father's height and bearing with that discerning ability to ooze confidence. But the physical resemblance ended there.

Zack's father bore his receding hairline without any attempt to cover the thinning spots with a comb-over or a toupee. His deeply lined face with its strong chin added to his stately handsomeness, along with a rich laugh and booming voice that caught and held her attention. Paul Keathley had a visible partnership with success on all fronts except with his son.

Naomi tried to think of something to say to alleviate the tension. "Um, I really do appreciate you inviting my grandmother and me to your home." Even though she wasn't a part of the family and didn't know the full dynamics, she found it difficult to take the quiet role. Besides, the family was growing on her with their effusive welcome and generosity.

"Think nothing of it." Frannie waved her hand. "I want to have a party."

"Party?" Zack's fork clattered against the plate. "Why?"

"What do you mean why? I want Naomi to know how much we appreciate her. I want our friends to know what she did."

"Oh, my, I really don't need this much attention," Naomi excused herself.

"Don't worry, Zack. Vernetta won't be invited." Chantelle's eyes sparkled with mischief.

"Vernetta? I don't care about Vernetta. Never did," Zack protested.

"Vernetta is a woman he lusted after through college," Chantelle explained to Naomi. "She eventually married a doctor, but now they're divorced. She's available again."

"Never liked that girl." Frannie wrinkled her nose. "She wore her morals like a—"

"Would both of you quit?" Zack tried to smile at her, but the contortion of his mouth looked as if he was in pain.

Now Naomi wanted to know more about Vernetta. What type of woman attracted Zack and didn't meet his mom's approval? She didn't want to be cast in that category.

Not that she would ever be Zack's woman.

"Naomi used to have some crazy men come after her too, especially being a professional athlete." Her grandmother piped up.

"Really?" Zack propped his elbows on the table.

Her grandmother beamed under everyone's attention. "One even found where *I* lived and left tons of flowers on the porch every night."

"For Naomi?" Chantelle had also joined in.

"No. For me. He figured that if he won me over that I would convince Naomi to give him a chance."

"And…" Zack never took his eyes off Naomi.

"Although I was flattered, my living room was looking like a funeral parlor."

"How did you get rid of him?"

"I told him that she was far gone in a relationship. And that I was heading off to meet her boyfriend's family in Washington."

Naomi's head snapped to look at her grandmother, who grinned with the innocence of a small child.

"Ha." Chantelle clapped her hands. "How convenient."

"Lucy, I like how you think." Zack's mother winked

at her grandmother. A small smirk worked at the corner of her mouth.

Actually, Naomi didn't quite see the comedy in the situation.

"Well, I don't know much about Naomi, but I like that white lie. Zack, now this is the type of woman who can sit at our dinner table." His father polished off the rest of his chicken.

"Grandma Lucy, you've got to stay for the party." Chantelle leaned over and hugged the older woman.

"Oh, I wish, sweetheart, but I've got my husband who depends on me." She explained his medical needs with dialysis and diabetes. "I trust that Naomi will relax and heal under your care."

"Definitely. She can stay as long as she wants."

"Oh, no, I couldn't. I'll be heading home."

"Home? In Chicago, where there is no one to take care of you?"

"I'm functioning just fine. See? I'm sitting up eating, moving around." She raised her hands to show off her mobility. The sharp pain in her side almost made her whimper, but she bit her lip and shoved the hurt aside.

"Maybe you should tell that to your body," Zack replied. "You're breaking out in a sweat."

"At least one more week, please?" Frannie asked.

"I can't possibly sit still for another week."

"Zack, would you be Naomi's companion while she's here?" Frannie asked.

"Would be one way to get him to visit more often," his father added.

"Fine," Zack said shortly.

"Oh, no, you're not going to sound as if I asked you to move a mountain. Where are your manners?" His mother glared at him.

"I didn't mean it that way." Zack set down his napkin.

He rested his folded arms on the table and leaned forward. His dark eyes practically drowned her in their mysterious gaze. Up close she admired the smoothness of his face and the strong lines that defined his features. But as always, his mouth drew her. Its wide strength covered immaculate, white, perfect teeth. She'd barely felt the fullness of his lips. As he was poised to speak, she couldn't help but focus her gaze on his mouth.

"I would be honored to serve as Naomi's companion during her stay. Will you stay?"

His question had been asked in a softer tone, almost in a husky whisper as if they were the only two in the room. Naomi nodded.

"Fantastic. Now I can stop worrying about my granddaughter." Grandma Lucy pushed aside her plate. "I can't wait to see what's for dessert."

Chapter 4

Later, after dinner, Naomi opted to relax in the living room rather than retire to her room. She didn't want to act like a patient. Her grandmother and Zack's mom had settled in the family room to yell at the TV as the evening's reality shows played.

Chantelle had left for the evening with a bunch of noisy friends. Her recent episode didn't affect her youthful exuberance. But it didn't stop the mounds of advice and warnings from every member of her circle—including Naomi. Naomi followed her instinct to give Chantelle her private cell number. She might not know Seattle, but she'd find her if another emergency arose. Zack had followed his father out of the dining room. Naomi could only assume that an intense conversation was about to take place between the two men.

A soft sound near her broke her out of her musings.

She opened her eyes and turned to see Zack easing himself into the love seat next to her.

"Sorry. I tried to let you sleep."

"I wasn't sleeping. Letting my mind get quiet."

"Do you meditate?"

"Not formally. I do like sitting in a quiet room and allowing my thoughts to flow uninhibited. It frees me. It's kinda hard to explain. And you?"

"I've studied various meditating techniques. Helps with my migraines." His phone buzzed at his hip. "Excuse me." He looked at the number displayed, but didn't answer the call. A scowl settled over his face.

"Work?"

"Yeah. It's nothing," he said dismissively.

She'd beg to differ but didn't think he wanted her assessment, no matter how accurate.

Zack returned the cell phone to his hip. Then he looked up at her. "You know, you don't have to stay if you don't want to."

His flat, matter-of-fact sentiment caught her by surprise. She sat up despite her body's protest. Where did this change come from? Unless she'd managed to let her silly imagination run earlier when he'd asked her to stay. Now he'd turned into a cool, crafty persona.

"Do you want me to stay?" Why did his opinion matter? But she couldn't stop herself from asking.

"I don't live here."

"What does that mean? If you lived here, you'd have something to say about me staying here?"

"Yes."

She gave a short laugh. "Oh, man, you are pretty accurate with your razor-sharp honesty."

Zack shrugged.

"If you lived here, what would you say?" Naomi pushed. Her irritation was building to anger.

"I'd say that you had to leave."

Naomi pushed up out of the chair. Pain be damned. "Why?"

He shrugged.

Naomi walked over to where he sat on the love seat. She leaned over, her anger escalating like a pot on the boil. His bland gaze didn't help her disposition.

"Have you changed your mind?" he asked.

"Changed my mind about what?"

"About staying." Then he grinned.

Naomi pulled up. Guess she had changed her mind. But there was a smug tug at his lips that caused her to frown. What was he playing at?

"I suspected that if I said that you had to do one thing, you'd pick the opposite. I don't know if it's a natural trait to be stubborn or you've saved that up for me. So when I suggested that you stay, you said no. When I said you should go, then you said you're staying."

"You…you think too much of yourself." He did manage to irritate her quite a bit.

"No, I recognize a kindred spirit when I see one."

"You must not have a lot of friends."

"Actually, I'm very selective with those around me," Zack explained. "You, for instance, I like you around me, and my family. I think you would be a good influence on Chantelle."

"You barely know me."

"Something that could be rectified if you chose to relax and spend a few days here. If you invited me to benefit from your hospitality, I wouldn't object."

She didn't doubt that he wouldn't object. His relaxed

pose against the love seat with one arm casually resting on the back of the seat invited her.

She could see herself sitting next to him, curled against his body, inhaling his expensive cologne while admiring his strong jawline as he uttered his sarcastic views on life. Really, she was the one who wouldn't object. The man had sex appeal for days. She had the appetite to appreciate its effect.

If she attached a calorie count to the overall visual stimulation, she'd have to check herself into a weight-management program. Despite his height and muscular frame, he moved with a casual elegance. Everything about him pulled her, drawing her interest with a tantalizing invitation—the velvet chocolate skin tone was a backdrop to piercing eyes hooded with thick eyebrows that subtly twitched with his varied expressions. The long line of his nose descended into a peak that begged for her finger to trace its strong outline. His square jawline helped frame the distinctive face, angled by the high sculpted cheekbones. Again and again, his mouth had its own power and strength to draw her attention. She took a deep breath with the constant mental refrain to be cool.

Without warning, he stood and held her arms. The playful expression vanished and he looked into her eyes. She struggled to rid her mind of the feel of his touch. Maybe she should stop looking into the dark eyes and allowing her thoughts to run a little too wild.

Her gaze brushed over his nose down to his full, wide mouth. All she wanted to do was kiss those lips. She wanted to touch them with her lips, her tongue.

His arms slid from her arms to around her body, ever so gently. He lowered his mouth to hers and after a moment's hesitation launched an all-out capture of her mouth. To have her imagination turn into a reality suited her fine. His kiss softly awakened her mouth with a buzz to the senses that didn't require an introduction. She kept her arms tucked in at her side, not wanting any pain to distract from the moment. While he softly attended to her mouth, she enjoyed the slight twitch of his muscles on her kneading touch. Her enjoyment was like a heady aftereffect from a good wine. She couldn't stop even if she wanted.

"You're beautiful," he remarked. He had to say something to give his body time to stand down.

"I know. So keep kissing me."

Her response drew his laugh. But he didn't wait to see if she was serious. If she thought he wouldn't follow through on her directive, then she didn't really understand him. She didn't realize that he wanted more than a stolen kiss or a brief unexpected acquaintance.

He kissed her with renewed passion, allowing his mouth to tell his story without words.

If he planned this correctly, the first thing he couldn't do was get caught getting fresh with his mother's guest. He drew away from the warmth of her lips. And because he couldn't help himself, added a final peck. "You've got to stop throwing yourself at me like that or I may get banished from the family kingdom."

"You are a devil with a lowercase *d*." She pushed away from him and he released her.

"I'll take that as a term of endearment." To eliminate his fixation on the empty feeling where she recently stood, he folded his arms. "I think we should reunite with the others, don't you?"

She straightened her hair and pulled at her shirt. Her eyes accused him but didn't hold any animosity. He sensed a rebuke forming, but he didn't allow her the opportunity to say anything. He walked ahead of her and then paused in the doorway for her to follow. As she walked past him, he lightly brushed her hair, which was tousled on the side. Then he dropped his hand balled into a fist.

His cell phone rang. The spell broke, especially when he saw who called. He mouthed "sorry" and headed off to a quiet area to have the not-so-nice discussion with his business partner.

In the meantime, she had to tell her grandma that she'd changed her mind. She'd be staying for another week. Somehow, she didn't think that her grandmother would object.

Zack headed back to his office, his face set in a grim mask of anger. His assistant met him at the door. She shook her head slightly. He picked up on the warning and didn't ask what was on her mind. Instead, he stepped into the waiting area and looked around expecting to see the businessman who gave him heartburn.

"Jamison is in the conference room," Rachel, his assistant, said.

He nodded and headed down the hallway. He opened the door and spied his business partner with another man. What was this all about?

"Hi, Zack. Let me introduce you to one of my colleagues, Seth Lassiter."

"Mr. Lassiter." Zack shook the proffered hand, trying to size up this new face. The squinty cast of his eyes, pinched features and weak chin didn't give him confidence. He decided to wait and let Jamison do the talking.

"Look," Jamison began. "I know you think that

things aren't going as fast as you expected. I, on the other hand, think that we are right on track. The city council is willing to stand down from making a decision about the types of stores that will fill the mall."

Zack held his response. Instead he looked pointedly at Lassiter.

"Oh, Lassiter will come in on the deal, my end of course. Can't hurt to have more capital."

"This is something that we should have discussed privately—no offense." He observed that the man barely blinked and stared back at him with the coldness of a robot.

"Mr. Keathley, I am a man of many connections. I know what this small town needs. Bring in the right businesses and you bring the high-end professionals."

"But this was supposed to be for the middle income, our targeted demographic."

"The middle draws the lower end. The upper income will draw the middle." He stroked his goatee, his actions full of slimy deliberation. "Look around at the megaplexes that have popped up over the state. They are overpopulated with a nagging criminal element that makes the lawyers and doctors run."

"I don't need another partner." Zack didn't bother to look at Lassiter.

"I beg to differ." Jamison opened his briefcase and pulled out a thick sheaf of papers. He slid the packet over to Zack. "Read it and get back to me. Twenty-four hours, okay?"

"What is this?" Zack skimmed the document, noting the legalese in various fonts. What was Jamison up to? From the first glance, the document looked like the paperwork they had signed between them. Now that this man sat in the room and Jamison insisted that they needed him, Zack had a sick feeling that he'd learn exactly what was happening when he poured through the document.

"We'll talk later." Jamison stood and adjusted his tie. He waited for Lassiter to stand next to him before addressing Zack. "I haven't tried to pull anything over on you. I've always said that we needed an additional partner to win over the council and to get the protesters to realize that they can't stop progress. The longer it takes for us to break ground, the more money I'm losing. That's not the business model that I'm interested in pursuing."

Zack didn't respond. He had nothing to say. Every word that Jamison uttered angered him, much less his so-called partner Lassiter. They sounded like sharks roving through unsuspecting victims. Many of the council members might buy into the skewed point of view and take a protectionist stance against the wrong kind of people moving in.

Although Zack had grown up in privileged circumstances, he could still remember his early days as a child whose mother had to give him up. Her unmarried state and lack of funds tossed him into an orphanage. No matter how well he was looked after, he didn't forget that he couldn't go home because he was a burden.

The Keathleys opened their hearts and home to him after they lived in Haiti. His adopted father got his start in the land development business when he helped with rebuilding a depressed area in the countryside, while his adopted mother volunteered in the orphanage. He knew they were special because of how loving they were to each other. But they also paid attention to him, talking to him as though his opinions really mattered.

Every day, his mother visited him until the orphanage

allowed him to go visit her. He loved staying in their house, which was so unlike the orphanage, with the house staff, clean, shiny surroundings and fresh smell to everything. For over year, he was tutored on his regular schoolwork, excelling in math. Back then, his father was proud of him.

Maybe he was being too hard on the old man. He probably was still proud, although his insistence on his following in his footsteps caused friction between them.

"Sir, will you be needing anything?" Rachel's voice interrupted his thoughts. "I'm going to head out now."

"No, Rachel, thank you, I'm fine. I'll lock up."

She paused, but looked as if she decided against speaking her mind. "Mr. Keathley, I hope you don't think that I'm overstepping, but…"

"It's okay. I know."

She nodded, turned and left him sitting at the conference table. The packet of the papers still remained in front of him. Very slowly he read and turned the page, continuing until the sun set behind the shuttered blinds.

"I think you're feeling better," Chantelle exclaimed as she hurried through the foyer toward the kitchen.

"I feel good." Naomi closed the front door after a short, enjoyable walk through the neighborhood. She couldn't bear to sit in the house idle. Frannie wouldn't let her do a thing. Plus she needed to exercise for when she had to return to the reality of her basketball life.

"I'm about to send out a mass e-vite to a few of my buds." Chantelle tossed over her shoulder. She plopped down in front of a laptop that was in a nook.

"Can I help?"

"Sure. Over there is my other laptop. Can you send out e-vites to this group?" Chantelle handed her a page filled with e-mail addresses.

"How many people are you inviting?" Naomi glanced down the list, figuring there were probably fifty addresses. Thank goodness Zack was able to stop his mother from issuing any invitations for her party.

Chantelle shrugged.

"Does your mother know?" Naomi could guess at that answer.

"It's no big deal. I'll buy a few pizzas. Somebody will bring the drinks and we'll hang out in the back. If it was warmer, we could have used the pool. I told Mom that we needed to enclose it."

"When are you planning to have the party?" Naomi considered herself a fast typist, but this long list might challenge her skills.

"Friday."

"Like in two days?" Naomi paused, waiting for Chantelle to correct her.

The young woman presented her usual shrug. She punched a key on the keyboard and leaned back with a huge grin. "All done. How are you doing over there?"

Naomi shook her head.

"Okay, while you do that, I'd better post a note to some folks' Wall."

"You think that's safe?"

"If they have my address, they'll know how to get here. And that's only to my friends. Plus it's not like I'm putting it in my status update. Do you think I'm clueless?"

Naomi wanted to say yes. Considering how close Chantelle had become with her, she didn't have a problem telling her what was on her mind. But she knew that Chantelle like to play the naïve card and blow off sound advice. She'd seen it done to her mother and to Zack. Watching Chantelle blow off Zack was more fun, though. He seemed unable to control his little sister. More often than not, he carried his frustrated frown with him whenever they were together.

After a half hour, Naomi said, "Okay, I'm done."

"Good. Now we have to go shopping." Chantelle led her out of the house. "I need a new outfit. I can't wait for my friends to meet you. So we can pick out a new outfit for you too."

Suddenly self-conscious, she looked down at her clothes. "What's wrong with what I'm wearing?"

Chantelle paused. "Do you really want to know? It's not…sexy."

Naomi rolled her eyes. "I don't need to be sexy. It's not like I'm picking up one of your young friends."

"No, silly, it's not for my friends. It's for my brother."

"What?" Naomi froze behind Chantelle who held up the car keys.

"I've decided that you would be good for him."

"I'm not a health tonic."

"Don't you think he's handsome?"

Naomi shrugged. Her pulse did its erratic dance, a new habit that occurred whenever she thought about the tall, sleek, arrogant man.

"Don't you want him? Lots of women want him, although I don't understand why they seem addicted to his negative personality."

"I think this conversation doesn't need to continue." Naomi pushed Chantelle out the door.

"Are you embarrassed? You need to become a modern woman. Say what's on your mind. If you feel the need to be with a certain man, then you should tell him, go after him. All this courtship stuff is for the old folks."

"Your dating habits are scary," Naomi said with warning in her voice.

"No, I'm being practical. If you wait or play games, you might end up being alone for a long time. Nothing wrong with being single, but why not have some fun while you're at it? I'm inviting a bunch of old boyfriends and potential ones. I decide who will be next."

"Alrighty, then." Naomi got into the car. Even with her sorority sisters, she didn't have to worry about their dating habits. Not that she considered herself a prude, but she'd like to have some conversation, some romance before going to bed with someone. She didn't believe it had to take a certain amount of time before something physical happened but according to Chantelle's theory, a one-night stand was not a bad thing.

"Back to my brother. Don't you want him?"

"I am not going to answer you. And I'm not going to talk about your brother."

"I know he irritates you, but he's not bad-looking. Plus I've seen him check you out. Boy, does he like to look at your butt. Every time you walked by, he'd look at you like you were a mouthwatering piece of chocolate."

Naomi blushed in waves, growing hotter and hotter. She couldn't adjust fast enough to Chantelle's candor, but she also couldn't react to the fact that Zack was checking her out.

"Plus the way he had you in a lip lock the other day, I was sure that you'd jump his bones by now."

Naomi opened her mouth to respond but closed it, deciding that she had no defense for her action and certainly no defense for her reaction that she couldn't wipe that moment from memory.

Jumping Zack's bones filled her thoughts.

Chapter 5

Friday arrived with an unusual burst of warm weather for October. The sun had center stage without clouds to mar its luminous presence.

Several long tables and benches covered the back lawn. Balloons decorated the porch where the pizza and other food items would be. The visible signs of a party in full effect.

Naomi had seen Chantelle's RSVP list. There was no way that everyone would stay outdoors. Her mother fussed but seemed to have caught Chantelle's giddiness, which defied logical discussion. And despite it all, Naomi looked forward to meeting her young friend's peers.

"Chantelle Keathley, what are you wearing?"

"Oh, please don't make a big deal, Mom. It's not like I'm wearing some skanky top or something."

"That could be debated." Frannie frowned as Chantelle sauntered past her.

Naomi would have loved to warn Frannie that her daughter had a tattoo on her hip. She'd seen the star when Chantelle modeled low-slung jeans. The cropped top was a deliberate addition so that the tat could play peek-a-boo. If she'd worn such a thing, her grandmother would have hit the roof, college girl or not. She remembered when in her freshman year of high school she got a friend to give her a second piercing in her ear what a big deal was made. Her grandfather had to intervene on her behalf. Otherwise, her grandmother would have made her take out the stud and allowed the hole to close.

Chantelle pulled out her cell phone and read the display window. "Looks like Stan and Brie are here."

Naomi didn't have to wait long before a mismatched couple emerged from the side of the house. Stan had the look of a dark Italian male model, while Brie was a very petite Asian girl with a Mohawk.

Naomi helped herself to a cup of punch. As other guests in various getups and strange adornments arrived, she got comfortable. Their exaggerated mannerisms and over-the-top enthusiasm for everything provided a wonderful viewing opportunity. And yet Naomi loved that Chantelle enjoyed life outside of any cookie-cutter style and mentality.

"Don't look longingly at them. They are kids with no sense of responsibility." Zack stood next to her.

"Whoa, don't you sound like a Grinch," she teased.

"Why is she having a party?"

"She felt like it." Naomi glanced up at the square jaw, but couldn't help noticing how his lips tightened into a flat line.

"I'm sure they didn't pay for a thing. As usual, she's

the one feeding her so-called friends. They just want to use her."

Naomi thought the same thing about Chantelle's so-called friends, but she wasn't so adamant with her conclusion.

"Who is that guy?"

Naomi looked in the direction of Zack's hand. She allowed his other hand to rest lightly on her forearm. She spied a young guy who dressed differently from the rest. He had a certain sophistication in his taste of pale blue polo shirt and olive-green khakis. He stood back from the crowd as if he were studying them.

A blonde girl came up from behind and slipped her arm around his waist in a playful hug. However, he pushed her hands away with a rough motion of disgust. Her hurt expression was lost on him. His intense gaze didn't include her.

"He's looking at Chantelle."

"I should have a talk with him." He moved forward.

"Ah…no." Naomi stepped forward to push Zack back. Her hands met the hard sheath of muscle under his shirt. The man didn't seem to have an ounce of fat. For a moment, she'd forgotten why she was standing face-to-face with him.

"I don't like the way he's looking at my little sister."

"I know. But you can't go and make a scene. You won't get what you want and you'll end up being the bad guy."

He shifted his focus from the offensive guy to her face. A small smile tugged at his mouth, providing a sexy tilt to his lips. "I didn't know you cared."

Naomi dropped her hands. The heat from touching

him still radiated in the palms of her hands. Then she remembered Chantelle's words about their attraction and she took a few steps back to break any romantic connection.

"Oh, here he comes." Zack turned toward the guy.

"No." Naomi lowered her voice. "I'll take care of it."

Puzzled, he looked at her. "How? And why?"

"Because I'm sure that I can find out his intentions and still save Chantelle from the embarrassment."

"That's not my priority." Zack's scrutiny hadn't wavered.

"Clearly, but she'd be mortified."

"Maybe she could learn a few tips from how I handle these bozo men."

"As much as I think you would do a fine job as a bouncer of a nightclub, this is her party. I have a tad more subtlety than you. Let me do my thing."

"This I have to see," Zack challenged.

Naomi strode over to the young man. She didn't have a clue what she'd say to him. But the mocking glint in Zack's eyes couldn't be ignored.

The man had moved closer to the pool. He continued his predatory surveillance of Chantelle. At any moment, she expected him to drop on all fours and scurry along the tables and benches in search of his prey.

"Hi, I'm Naomi."

"The basketball girl," he acknowledged.

"Are you having a good time?"

"Not my crowd."

"Why are you here, then?"

"I came with my boys."

"Really." Naomi made a show of scanning the area for a cluster of frat boys.

"Look. I'm not into older women," he said dismissively.

"No, you're into girls with trust funds," Naomi countered.

"What?" He moved away from her. The blonde ran over to hook arms with him again. He pulled away for the second time. "Back off," he told her. He stalked away.

"This guy is a piece of work," Naomi muttered. She looked at Chantelle laughing and chatting with her odd assortment of friends. This guy clearly wasn't a part of that, nor did he have the personality to join them. Like an animal, he stayed on the outskirts waiting for the opening when he could get Chantelle's attention. Knowing her quirks, the young girl was likely to feel flattered and up for the challenge of conquering this new game.

Naomi decided that would not happen, not today, not on her watch. She followed the guy and inserted herself between him and his woman or whatever she was.

"You really want me, don't you?" he said sarcastically.

"Yeah, I do," Naomi flirted. "Why don't you come with me?"

He followed her around to the front of the house.

"Which one is your car?"

"Uh-oh, a freak. You sure you can handle what I've got to give?" He grinned. "My car is over there."

The tricked-out Corvette sparkled under the sun with its fire-red paint job. The vehicle screamed babe magnet. The tires gleamed jet-black with shiny chrome wheels. Obviously the car was the guy's true girlfriend. Pride bounced off his chest as he approached his car.

Naomi eased her hip on the hood and propped her weight with her foot against the side of the car.

"What the hell?"

"Shut up. I'm only going to say this once. You aren't staying at this party any longer. Don't bother contacting Chantelle. If I think you are trying to go around me, I will come after you. I've dropped opponents bigger than you." She pushed off from the car to close the gap between them.

He looked up and tried to hold the stare, but took a step back. His eyes grew dark, but nothing about his face scared her. Protecting people she cared about always brought out the fierce loyalty in her. Her sorority sisters had to deal with her overprotective nature. Now Chantelle had earned her attention. She wanted any reason to clock this guy in the chin.

"Don't even think about it."

Naomi didn't have to turn to feel Zack's looming presence. She had the courage to go toe-to-toe with this fiend, but having Zack as reinforcement made her stand a little more erect.

The guy wilted, much of his earlier bravado escaping from his body like a leaky valve. He didn't waste any time hurrying around the rear of the car, looking as if he wanted to avoid contact with Zack. The roar of the engine punctuated his retreat as he reversed and headed off the property.

Naomi grinned. "Now that was fun," she said. Good thing Chantelle hadn't seen her intervention. She doubted that the girl would understand that she'd done what she did for her benefit.

"I think we make a good team," Zack proclaimed.

"Heck, I think we make an awesome team." Naomi

smiled at Zack. After their minor tug of war, she enjoyed the thaw between them.

"Let's get out of here." He clasped his hand in hers and headed to his car.

Naomi didn't hesitate. Chantelle would be fine. They'd taken care of the greatest threat. Now, with her adrenaline still pumping, she was game for another adventure. This time, she'd have a man who filled her mind with scandalous thoughts and fantasies.

Sitting next to Zack in his sleek luxury sports car, Naomi relaxed and enjoyed the speedy entry into the traffic. She gazed out at the traffic and night bustle that marked the beginning of the weekend. So many of her evenings were spent in practice or playing a game. Her dating life was a spurt here and there. Many times, she ended a budding relationship because her focus couldn't be divided or prioritized. Basketball always came at the top.

"You're awfully quiet."

"I haven't had a chance to sit back and breathe."

"How's the recovery going?"

"It's going. The muscles across my ribs are healing, and I'm a bit stiff."

"You miss the team, don't you?"

"Sometimes." Even as she said the truth, the guilt for not thinking about her teammates, practice, the game unsettled her.

"Not that I think what happened to you is a good thing. But I do feel that you now have time to yourself. That's not bad."

"And are you following your own advice?" Naomi pushed back. She didn't want Zack trampling through her thoughts. At least not in that gentle, caring voice.

"No, but I'm good at helping others," he joked. "Ready for food?"

"I was eyeing the pepperoni, green pepper and onions pizza—but I got sidetracked with my bouncer duties."

"Well thank goodness you didn't have any. I'd have to give you a breath mint before I kissed you."

Immediately the blood surged to her face as if on cue. She stared ahead, trying to focus on the vanity plate on the car in front of them—IMASTUD. All the small license plate needed was neon lights with an arrow pointing to Zack.

"You want me to kiss you."

"No." She looked at him firmly. "And no means no."

"Okay. Your wish is my command." He grinned at her. "Remember that."

Somehow she wondered how he'd managed to make her feel as if he'd deftly moved her out of the driver's seat. Yet she was up for the challenge—maybe. A little flirtation never hurt anyone, did it?

"We're here." Zack pulled into a high-rise that was firmly along the lakefront.

"Home?"

"Yep. Eventually I'll get a house. But for my lifestyle, this works."

"As the rich playboy of Washington State."

"Or the serious-minded businessman."

"Must be from what side of the fence you're on."

"I'd like you to join me on this side." He opened her car door and extended his hand to assist.

"Only for a while. My grandmother warned me about men like you."

"Your grandmother loves me."

"Why? 'Cause you flattered her?" She sized him up

as they walked to the doorway. Chances were that her grandmother would like him. The doorman opened the door and touched his cap with his gloved hand.

"She told me to take good care of you when she left. I promised to do my part to make you comfortable."

"Hmmm," she said with a smile. "You'll have a short time frame for that. I'm heading out in a week."

"Really?" Zack's eyebrow shot up in a questioning peak. "That sounds definite."

"It's more than talk." She frowned and waited for him to enter the elevator before she followed. "What do you have up your sleeve?"

"Nothing," he said slyly. "Well, actually that's not true. My family is heavily involved in the local chamber of commerce. There is a fundraising reception that will donate to local soup kitchens in time for Thanksgiving meals. If nothing I said convinces you, then let me say that my mother would love to have you there."

She watched him slide his card into the slot above the buttons for the floors and hit the PH button. As the elevator cab shot smoothly up the length of the building, Naomi felt as if her feelings for Zack were on an express ride to some unknown peak.

"Are you thinking about it?"

"I'm trying to overcome the horror of me going to anything that requires heels, sequins and random conversation. I'm so not that type." Naomi shook her head for emphasis.

"I think you'd clean up just fine. You'll be on my arm, so no need for conversation."

"Why, the women you date aren't there for conversation?"

"Oh, now that had a bite." He playfully winced. "I don't have time to date. What I do is pretty important to me. I find many women too clingy and with a preset agenda to fix me."

She laughed. "Which usually ends in disaster?"

Zack nodded. "I don't see you as clingy and trying to fix me."

The elevator doors opened and there were four doors visible, two on one side of the hallway and the other two on the other. Zack walked to the far right and punched in his code. She expected the door to open like those in the *Star Trek* shows given the high-end technology required to enter. Instead he pushed open the door and stepped aside for her to enter.

"From the looks of things, I don't think you have to worry about being fixed. You seem to have everything you want or are capable of getting whatever you want."

Proof of his success surrounded her in the penthouse suite, with its large living area that stretched across the side of the building to where the floor-to-ceiling windows looked out on the Pacific Ocean.

The furniture arranged in exact square formation were leather and chrome with beige and natural colors. The color scheme broke pattern with occasional splashes of cranberry.

"May I fix you a drink?"

"I'll take a soda." Naomi watched him push a button for the bar to slide out toward him. He grabbed a glass and tossed in the ice cubes. The way he moved to get her drink was smooth, unlike the nervous jitters that she had right now. He seemed completely oblivious to what he was doing to her. She didn't need liquor to cloud her thinking as she took the cool beverage from him.

"Have a seat."

"I thought you were going to feed me," she said, tension evident in her voice.

"I do plan to feed you. You'll help me with the process."

"Guess we aren't going to a restaurant."

"No. I've got a different evening planned."

"You're reminding me of that guy we kicked out today."

"I hope not. I'm not stalking you, nor am I doing anything against your will. You'll let me know when you're ready to leave."

"Okay."

"So tonight's agenda will be to fix dinner, enjoy the meal, watch a movie or talk. Then I'll go to my room and you can go to the guest room—unless you choose otherwise," he said seductively. "I do like a surprise."

"Are you drunk?"

He smiled. "No, not yet."

"Your mother is expecting me back at the house. I don't have clothes. But that's beside the point. I'm not staying."

"You *are* a nervous one. So the calm, kick-ass persona is just a facade? Interesting," he said, almost as if to himself. "My mother knows you're with me—actually, she encouraged it. She thought that I was being a good son to volunteer to take you under my wing for the weekend. As for clothes, Chantelle packed your clothes before the party. I had someone bring your suitcase. You're all set." He unbuttoned the top buttons of his shirt. "Excuse me, but I've got to get comfortable. Making stir-fry could get hot."

"Zack. Zack!" She wasn't about to let him ignore her. She hurried after him, following close on his heels through another doorway.

He halted, causing her to bump into him. He turned and casually wrapped his arm around her, holding the small of her back. His shirt had flown open and her palms rested on his bare chest, skin to skin. The fragrance of his cologne gently teased her, echoing its sexy owner's arrogance.

"What's the matter? You look worried."

"Stop playing games, Zack." Her voice was high-pitched.

He pulled her closer. She felt the strong heart beating under her palm. Her head could tuck easily under his chin. Although she had the height, he managed to make her feel light and graceful.

"I would never play games with you. You're too special. You've earned my utmost respect for what you did for Chantelle. In my line of business, I have to learn to read people. I know that you would love to drop the sense and sensibilities and enjoy life."

"You make the most illogical stuff sound just right," she said softly.

"I do have the ability to charm with words." He kissed her and then pulled back to look at her. "I also have the ability to charm with some other natural talents." He grinned.

Naomi had to laugh. Although he was pushing hard to seduce her, she wasn't offended. A part of her wanted to match him, flirt for flirt, wit for wit, anything he thought she couldn't handle, she welcomed the challenge.

His mouth covered hers again.

Zack pulled her up with a soft growl deep in his throat. Careful of her injuries, he gently tightened his arms around her body. He wanted to kiss her into submission, but resisted. As much as he threw out his macho declarations, he hoped that she would stay. He could be the perfect gentleman, but he'd rather not be that.

Her lips teased him with their own response to his attention. Contact with her mouth caused his body temperature to soar. Yet when he followed the invitation of her partly opened mouth, he swept across her tongue.

Static electricity might as well have shot through his veins. The instant attraction took root from the soles of his feet up through his body to the source of his pleasure.

He brought his hands to the side of her face and cupped her ever so gently. He looked into her eyes and the swollen lips.

"Ask me to stay," Naomi said breathlessly.

"Stay."

Her eyebrow raised.

Understanding spread through his stubborn brain. "Please. Stay."

She nodded. Then she slid her hand around the back of his head and guided him back to her mouth. Stunned, he had nothing to say, but words didn't matter at a time like this. She pushed his shirt down off his shoulders. He struggled to get out of the offending garment. But the shirt wouldn't budge over the cuff links.

She pushed him back into the room until the back of his legs pressed against the bed. Then with a heavy push of her hand, he fell back on top of his comforter. He tried to speak, but so much was happening so fast that he could only concentrate on not making himself look like a fool.

"Are you sure you're ready for this?"

"Looking forward to it."

"You've been taunting me. Careful what you ask for."

Here was one woman who didn't step aside. Her strength turned him on.

She straddled him, resting lightly on his hips. A dangerous place to be, but she would relish the painful restraint it caused him. Wicked woman.

"You know you can't be the only one on top," he said, a touch out breath.

"A man who doesn't know how to sit back and enjoy the ride. Amazing," she said lightly. She ran her hands up his chest up to his neck. He almost growled when her lips trailed a similar path over his rib cage, over his chest and up to his neck.

Maybe she'd see the pulse at the base of his neck, because his heartbeat sounded loud to his own ears. If he could distract his mind for a bit, his breathing could settle. But the more she planted feathery kisses along his chin to the corner of his mouth, the more he fought the urge to start hyperventilating.

His hands clamped down on her hips to keep her still. The grinding motion stirred his emotions into a rich brew of sinful ideas for this woman.

When her tongue traced the opening where his lips parted, his hands betrayed him with their possessive grab on either side of her behind. Her lean physique didn't compromise her muscular buttocks. He pulled her toward him.

His mouth opened to her attention like a willing student. He'd like to discover what Naomi could teach him.

"I want to see you," he said when she threw her head back for air.

"You're not paying attention to the rules." She reached back and cupped him.

He almost squeaked. His leg twitched.

Her hand stroked him, once.

"I'm trying to remember the rules." He really was trying to remember what he was supposed to recall.

She moved her hand back down over his arousal and as added torture gently rubbed him in a circular motion.

His hips raised, but he saw no mercy in her face. He tried to toss her off his legs, but she managed to hang on by hooking her feet under him.

She took his hand and placed it under her shirt against her stomach. "We'll wait until you come up with the right answer."

He growled again. "I can't take much more of this. You're trying to kill me."

"You're a big boy—and I mean that literally." She gazed at his body. "I don't do well with orders."

"Please." He dragged the word out.

"Exactly." She took his hand and ran it over her bra.

He touched the smooth fabric that had proved a nuisance when he was a high school senior. Through its smooth silken cover, he felt her nipple harden.

He felt her thighs tighten around him. Good. She also fought the onslaught of arousal that almost left him debilitated.

Her hand only lightly stayed on his. He slid under the stiffness below the bra cup to slip his hand over the soft mound. Touching only satisfied one sense. He wanted to see. Taste.

"Please take off your shirt."

She nodded, then pulled off her shirt and tossed it on

the other side of the bed. He liked that she wasn't shy about her athletic body. Her hands relaxed at her sides as she took in the array of expressions that flitted across his face.

"You're beautiful."

He unsnapped her bra and waited for her to remove the delicate contraption. Her breasts greeted him, nipples puckered and at attention. He pulled her to him until he could reach up for a nipple.

Nectar of the gods couldn't have been any sweeter. His tongue twirled around the sensitive skin, lathing it with the attention that he deemed necessary.

He saved her nipple for last, only blowing on it to heighten the sensation. When he covered his mouth over the sensitive bud, the nipple tightened even more.

A small cry of pleasure escaped as Naomi threw back her head. While he played with her breast, she kneaded him to a firm arousal. He wanted her now.

"Allow me to get a condom." He opened his night drawer and grabbed the necessary protection. He slipped it on and returned his attention.

"Don't even think about it. You don't get to be on top." Naomi pushed him back on the bed before lowering herself onto him.

He stilled her motion with his fingers in a steely grasp around her hips. The warmth of her body encased his arousal in sensual capture.

Staying true to his promise, he followed her rhythm. The slow grind drew him up, and then she eased off to relax him a bit. The movement repeated with gradual intensity and slight frequency.

Too late. He couldn't keep the grunts from emanating into the air. He needed every bit of energy as she squeezed him with her walls, contracting and relaxing along his shaft. He gritted his teeth.

"Do it with me."

"You don't have to tell me twice." They created a heat between them as if they had a burner under them pushing them to that boiling point. Everything within him surged forth with a speed and force that bore no retreat.

He felt her pause and her body began to quiver. Not waiting any longer, even if he'd wanted to, his release came in waves to the beat of his frantic pulse.

In response, her body answered the call like an incoming tide rolling and receding. Together they clung to each other coasting on the edges of reason while their bodies finished out the symphony that their lovemaking had started.

Her head rested against his chin. The citrus scent from her hair soothed him. She stayed in his arm molded against his frame. Their worlds had come together in set of circumstances that could only have been destiny. After their many conversations, he'd learned that they had more in common than he'd thought. Zack wanted her almost like a soul mate. He hoped that she didn't regret any minute of this. Frankly, he wanted seconds.

Chapter 6

Naomi cleaned up and repaired her hairdo before emerging. She didn't want to think about her bold actions with Zack. The memories were too new and stark now that reality kicked into her consciousness. Worse yet, she didn't regret one moment.

But what did this mean now? She still had to leave his family's home and go back to her world, her career. There couldn't be anything to come of this. Once Zack understood there was no future together, then she'd feel better.

As she dressed, she could hear the pots and pans being used in the kitchen. Now she had to walk out and join him for dinner. What to say? She controlled her panic and went to the kitchen.

"Ready for your cooking lesson?" Zack asked her while chopping onions.

"What's for dinner?"

"I switched from stir-fry to spaghetti."

"Ummm…I'm a little starved."

"Trust me. It'll be fun and then you'll get to enjoy your efforts."

She didn't want to talk about trust, even if it was only about food. Having something to take the attention off an uncomfortable situation was ideal. She could bury her head in the spaghetti sauce for the next hour.

"If you'd like a glass of white wine, check the refrigerator."

"Sounds good." The wine would help calm her nerves.

"Well, how about pouring a glass for me? Glasses are over there." He motioned toward the cupboard.

She poured the wine for them and watched him take a long sip. Why on earth was he acting like nothing unusual had just happened? Her desires had taken control over common sense. This required a major discussion. She couldn't let it happen again. He couldn't think that she lived the stereotypical life of a professional athlete, sleeping with anyone at each destination point.

"Earth to Naomi. I need the eggs, olive oil and another garlic clove."

Naomi snapped back to the present and followed Zack's instructions. She lined up all the items next to the other ingredients. Any time his hand came close to hers, she pulled back. Right now her senses were supersensitive. She didn't need him touching her. She didn't trust herself to be strong and withstand his sexy charm.

"I won't bite."

"I think I'd beg to differ." She'd had to check her neck to make sure there was no hickey on her neck as if she was a high school girl. Everywhere his mouth had touched her felt as if it had been the recipient of an erotic exploration.

"You look embarrassed. Don't be."

Naomi didn't answer. She'd let the blush that heated her face speak for itself.

"We enjoyed each other like adults…"

"Let's not talk about it," Naomi interrupted.

"Okay." He touched her hand. "But I want you to know that I have no regrets."

"Despite my tendencies on the wild side, a one-night stand was never on the list." Naomi planted her hands on the counter.

"That's good. I didn't figure us to be a one-night stand. Now stop distracting me. We need to get all this into the pot."

Naomi followed Zack's lead in cutting onions, garlic and mushrooms. Before long the savory odor of rich tomato sauce enhanced with oregano, basil and fresh parsley scented the air. Hunger pangs sounded as the bubbling sauce simmered under low flame.

"Next is the pasta."

"Not my forte. I always manage to undercook or overcook."

"You're refreshingly honest." Zack suddenly leaned forward and kissed her squarely on the lips.

She continually had to struggle to maintain control. "How's the pasta coming?"

"Just a few more minutes and it's all done." Zack's pride in his pasta-cooking skills radiated as a wide smile on his face.

"I'll get the table ready." Naomi set out the plates and the cutlery.

"Here are matches." Zack tossed a book to her.

Naomi noticed the brand-new candles in the silver-plated sconces. She'd also ignored them. Dinner with candles added a romantic touch that she wasn't sure she wanted to encourage.

She watched Zack approach the table with a large dish of pasta with the bright red spaghetti meat sauce liberally covering the top. He set it down between the plates, then waited for her to sit.

"Let's dig in," Zack prompted.

"I'll say Grace."

"Of course." Zack lowered his chin to his chest.

Naomi reached across the table for Zack's hand. She said the childhood prayer that her grandmother had taught her. When she raised her head afterward, she was pleased to see that Zack seemed to be adding his silent prayer, too.

"I think that I'm going to be quite spoiled by the time I leave. Actual home-cooked food is something I don't have time to enjoy. This is fantastic." She pointed with her fork at her meal, already half gone.

"Do I detect a tone of regret?"

"Sorry, didn't mean to sound whiney."

"You're being hard on yourself. But I think that you probably are an expert on that."

"I work hard for what I want, if that's what you mean." She leaned back and pushed her empty plate aside. The Chianti had relaxed her guard a little. "Once I've met a challenge, I tend to look for the next thing."

"You've reached that wall in your life."

"You can say that. Basketball is my life. My life is basketball."

"No man in the wings waiting for you?"

Naomi shook her head. She detected the deeper curiosity behind the question. She didn't care to be under anyone's microscope. She'd turned the mirror on her life once too often. Unlike her sorority sisters, she didn't have a husband or boyfriend. She didn't even have an occasional date. When she was playing basketball, she was practicing or working with her personal trainer. Her last boyfriend, over a year ago, had put himself in the position for her to pick between the game and him. The decision wasn't hard.

"Well, while you're here, I want you to enjoy the other side of life."

"That's what I'm afraid of doing. Enjoying a little too much."

"Even Cinderella followed her temptation," he said with a smile.

"There were repercussions, though."

"And a happy ending."

"I don't think Seattle, Washington, will be my ending."

"I hope to prove you wrong." Zack winked at her.

Naomi drained her second glass of wine. This man's flirtation with her was having an effect. Every statement made with sexy deliberation unraveled her desire to rebuild her defenses.

"Want to see the sun set?" Zack pushed back from the table and made his way behind her chair. His fingers stroked her shoulders, sending her nerves in a frenzy. "The sunset is beautiful from the balcony."

Naomi accompanied Zack onto the roof garden. She'd noted the area when he provided a tour of his condo. Until she stood outside, well above the other buildings in the immediate area, she'd had no idea of the view.

The clear view of the Pacific Ocean shimmered with jeweled tones. The fading sun projected deep splashes of violet, amber and silver over the choppy surface. Boats of various sizes sliced through the water heading in and out of port.

Sitting on top of the world gave Naomi a certain perspective. She felt free with the wind rustling her hair and completely relaxing her body.

"Here, I brought the remainder of the wine." Zack handed her a fresh glass and then poured a generous amount into the wide vessel.

"Thank you." Naomi set her glass to one side. Her head already felt loopy. Every time she looked into Zack's eyes, she couldn't promise not to become a blithering idiot.

Naomi turned her back on the view. Instead she stood with her back against the railing, waiting for Zack to top off his glass and join her. She loved watching him, studying the silent grace in everything he did. From the tilt of his head to the casual lift of the corner of his mouth, to the wide shoulders that always looked strong and decidedly masculine under a designer jacket, to his lean, chiseled physique, and to his long legs that propelled him forward with a power that caught anyone's eyes.

"We've been talking about me for most of the night." Naomi paused. "Who is Zack Keathley?"

"I'm a simple businessman."

Naomi waited. There was nothing simple about Zack. Some people had charisma and that it factor that made people want to be with them. Zack had a megadose of a magical element that without much effort exuded the power to draw attention. No way that he didn't have a slew of women ready to have their own *Survivor* game to fight for him like a piece of underpriced property.

"I'm hard at work building my business-development

company. All my energy goes there. The other part of my energy goes to Chantelle," he joked.

"You're part of the family's business?"

"No, I chose to do this on my own. I want to earn my wings. I enjoy being my own boss, making my own decisions, taking the risks."

"But it would be easier to lean on what your father has built."

"Exactly. I don't want to lean on anyone." Determination underlined his words. "I've been enough of a burden."

"Why so hard on yourself?" Naomi touched his cheek. The tension in his jaw worked under her hand. "I hardly think that anyone in your family sees you as a burden."

He pulled away from her. "Didn't mean to sound—"

"No," she interrupted. "I'm sorry. I'm stepping into your private life." She lowered her hand to give him back his personal space.

Zack took a moment before he spoke again. "I'm adopted. It was never a big family secret. I was almost five years old when I came to live with my parents. My dad had many lean years when he first started to build his company. Adoptions are expensive. I went to private schools, had tutors, all the things that add up." Zack stopped, his gaze averted. His mouth drew into a tight straight line as the memory of his painful past reflected in the squint of his gaze.

"I think it shows how much they love you. They wanted the best for you."

"I know," he admitted with a sigh. "But now I want to show them that I can be successful. I can support them and make them proud."

"Okay," Naomi said in a tone that indicated he was being ridiculous. "You're not realizing that your parents, even Chantelle, are proud of you. When you have your own family, you'll understand why they did what they did."

"A family of my own?" He snorted.

"That translates to a *no*, right?"

"I don't mind settling down," he said looking into her eyes. "But…"

"No kids? Not that you have to have kids. But I'm surprised that you're so adamant."

"Do *you* want children? Did you have a priority check with a children versus basketball moment?"

Naomi shrugged. "I postponed it. I didn't rule it out of my life"

"Right now, I'm focused on my business and finding out about my birth family."

"Are you looking for the reason behind your adoption?"

"I hear the doubt in your tone. I'm not a foolish romantic. I do have vague memories of my mother. Maybe she wonders what happened."

"What if you can't find her? Or if she's moved on?"

Zack shrugged. He pulled her into his embrace, then turned her toward the sunset. "We're missing it."

He was right. The sun now hovered lightly over the horizon. Long, thin clouds added horizontal lines along the orb. Temperatures dipped, especially as they stood out on the garden. Naomi nestled closer against Zack's chest.

"We should go inside," Zack suggested.

"It's quite beautiful."

"I didn't mean to get deep and dark. You do that to me," he said with a smile.

"I appreciate your honesty. I mean it."

"Even if you don't approve?"

"I try not to sit in judgment, because I may not live up to similar scrutiny."

He raised her chin with the crook of his finger. "I seriously doubt that." He kissed her lips with a tender touch before letting her go. "Let's make hot chocolate and watch a movie. Then I'll take you home."

"Sorry, but you see, now you're telling me what to do. So I have to say no, and do the opposite. I'm going to stay tonight. With you." She pulled him into the room that was hers for the evening. "Let's skip the hot chocolate."

Naomi entered the bedroom first, scanning the contents and noting the pristine condition. Her small suitcase was placed on a luggage rack. The premeditated act gave her pause.

"I've never used this bedroom. Nor have I ever asked my sister to pack a suitcase on a woman's behalf."

"Good. I'd hate to be a foregone conclusion." Naomi unzipped the suitcase and sifted through the contents, checking off all the necessary items to make her overnight stay comfortable.

"If you need anything, I can get it."

"I'm fine." She looked toward one of several doors in the room. "I'll hop into the shower."

"I'll go make that hot chocolate."

Naomi didn't say anything. He'd done a good job predicting her needs. Maybe he'd figure out the appropriate next move. After he closed the door, she undressed and donned a thick, luxurious robe that hung in a closet. The soft material warmed her body with a coziness that felt good. However, her body craved a hot shower.

She guessed at which door to open, picking the one closest to the wall.

"Oh, my goodness gracious!" She entered a large space that had the area to serve as another bedroom suite.

The bathroom probably rivaled a Roman bath with all the modern conveniences and then some. The honey-almond color offered a warm invitation with its copper-toned sink and oversize tub. She wished that she had time to take a soak, but she'd settled for the shower, which featured a large showerhead and four additional spouts. The thought of having the water hit her body all over enticed her. She threw aside the robe and stepped into the glass-enclosed stall before quickly turning on the water.

Water cascaded over her head, soaking her hair before bathing her entire frame. The jets of water shot out with a massaging pulse against her muscles. She closed her eyes to enjoy the watery treat.

"May I join you?"

Naomi jumped but immediately opened the shower door for Zack's entry. Despite the fact that she was naked, she was acutely aware that he was also naked. She boldly soaked up his beautiful physique.

"I'll do that." He took the small washcloth from her hands and flipped it over a towel bar. "I can do a better job with my hands."

She nodded. His hands against her body heated up her inner vibes. Zack had a knack for making her feel sexy with a glance, a brush with his fingers, or in this case, simply standing two inches from her.

Suddenly her throat felt dry. She leaned her head back

and allowed the water to trickle into her mouth. Then he kissed the side of her neck. She almost drowned, whether from the water or from her nerves awakening under the sensual waves rolling through her body.

His fingers played with her hair, sliding the strands behind her ear. He delivered another scorching kiss to her mouth. She didn't mean to but couldn't help digging her nails into his back. His mouth claimed hers with no hesitation. His desire spoke its own language, full of sensual hunger and passion.

She heeded his call with her own demand for his erotic touch in her most sensitive sweet spots. No words were necessary as she pressed against his muscular frame.

His tongue danced and stroked her mouth, conquering, dominating, taking possession of her willing mouth. But she wanted that seeking tongue to bathe her, play with her, stir her into a frenzy. With her back against the cool tile, she guided his face to her breasts, which perked up with anticipation.

When his mouth descended on her nipple, she swore that she momentarily zoomed into another dimension. She hooked him with a leg, pinning him to her as he continued to introduce his tongue down the length of her body.

She wanted to exclaim but couldn't. Her mouth opened, but only to moan as he tenderly kissed around her belly button. She pinned her hands against the tiles for some type of anchor. When he gently parted her legs, she did cry out. Her inner thighs trembled as his fingers meandered toward the apex of her legs.

Then he touched her with a slight brush of his fingertips, as if introducing himself to the sensitive lips. He stroked, stirring up her response to a rapid boil. She didn't think he could be so cruel as to play with her opening, skirting the area with a teasing touch.

Yet he upped the stakes when he accompanied his probing fingers with his tongue.

She hissed. Her mind no longer pretended to keep a coherent thought. Zack had managed to send her body into Defcon 3.

"Don't hold back, honey."

"I want you inside me."

He kissed her and sucked her folds with a suction that drove her to stand on her tiptoes.

"Please," she begged.

His fingers replaced his tongue. She knew where he was headed, his fingers slid along her walls to the destination that he probed with soft pressure.

"I can barely hold on." The air in her lungs felt as if in short supply.

"I don't want you to." He flicked her clit with his tongue. "There will be time for me to pleasure you in other ways."

Without warning, he increased the friction inside her. Her moans grew louder. Her hands grabbed his head. She wanted to cry out for him to stop but also to scream for him to continue. Her body arched, straining against the last remnants of control.

"You're stubborn." Zack kissed her inner thigh.

Well, that did it. Her release coerced by her complete surrender shook her body until she had to close her eyes. She had to let out the guttural scream. She had to stay on her tip-toes until the last pulsing orgasm throbbed to cessation.

As a finale, Zack kissed her gently between her legs.

Chapter 7

"I hope you're not going to the event like that." Chantelle hovered in the doorway with her hand on her hip.

Naomi looked down at her dress. The long midnight-blue dress with silver edging carried a high-end designer's name. She looked up at the younger woman. She was already nervous. Chantelle's critique didn't help.

"You look plain. Nice body and all, but we've got to brighten you up. I'll go get my makeup."

"Aren't you supposed to be leaving?"

"Yeah, but you're a fashion emergency." Chantelle hurried down the hallway still loudly exclaiming her disgust.

Naomi spun around in front of the full-length mirror, examining each angle. Frannie had accompanied her on the shopping spree, delighted that she'd agreed to stay and attend their fundraiser. She'd only agreed to wear this dress over the pantsuit choice if Frannie allowed her to pay.

"Okay, sit down over here near the lights." Chantelle produced an oversize compact of every color imaginable.

"I don't want to look like a paid escort." Naomi looked at some of the extreme shadings with distaste.

"Trust me."

Naomi raised an eyebrow as her eyes scanned Chantelle's face, noting the eyeliner that seemed too thick, the fake lashes that made her look in constant surprise and the glossy lips.

"Close your eyes. You don't have much time. I heard Mom downstairs getting on Dad's case because she's ready to go."

"I'm not going with them." Naomi fought the urge to open her eyes as the eye shadow was applied with swift strokes.

"Oh. Is my dear brother coming to take you to the fundraiser? I may have to stick around to keep an eye on both of you."

"You've done enough already." Naomi had dodged all Chantelle's questions about her overnight stay. She knew that her blushing didn't help.

"Naomi! Zack's here."

"Coming!" Naomi responded.

"Keep still for a few more minutes. I'm almost done. You need a killer lip color to add the final touch to my masterpiece." Chantelle took a step back and handed her a mirror. "Darn it, I'm good."

Naomi looked at her reflection and was stunned into silence. The face staring back at her bore little resemblance to her plain face with its sharp angles and prominent features.

"Knock 'em dead." Chantelle hugged her tightly. "I'm going to miss you. I hope you keep in touch."

"I promise. You go be a good student and don't give those professors a hard time."

After Chantelle left, Naomi turned to the bigger mirror and examined her appearance one last time before she headed downstairs. Now they would be going out officially as a couple. A short-term assignation that she knew would end the day she left Washington.

"You look fantastic." Zack whistled softly. "That gown is stunning. It's hugging you in all the right places."

"You look like you're going to make a meal of me."

"That's not quite what I'm going for." He grinned with pure, sexy mischief.

The gala event attracted the press and the upper-income social strata. Naomi used her mental calming exercises as they pulled up in front of the entrance. She waited for Zack to open her door to make sure that she had him at her side.

She'd been afraid that she was overdressed and the makeup too dramatic. The women put those thoughts to shame. She silently thanked Chantelle for the finishing touches.

"Shall we?" Zack rested his hand on her lower back.

Naomi walked through the entrance, noting the curious glances cast her way. She was with an eligible bachelor. "I think that I may be an impediment to many women's plans for you."

"Too bad for them." Zack's hand slid purposefully

along her back, settling on her hip. "Maybe I should leave no doubts." He kissed her neck. "You smell good."

"Stop. Everyone is watching, even the reporters." Naomi stepped away from him. "I think they want to talk to you."

Zack didn't appear interested in being cornered by any reporter. The photographers, on the other hand, didn't seem concerned with getting an interview. Instead, they photographed every angle as they crossed the entrance to the event.

Inside, the noisy din from outside was replaced with the music of an orchestra and several people already on the dance floor.

"Let's mingle a bit, and then I'm going to whip you around the dance floor."

"Whoa. I can do a lot of things. Dancing isn't one of them."

"That's because you haven't had a partner like me." He wiggled his eyebrows.

"No argument there."

Zack lived up to his promise, introducing her to businesspeople. All the names ran together. She knew her presence drew curious glances and pointed questions, but she stuck close to Zack to avoid any mini interviews. Her plan didn't stop the cameras from snapping in her face. She was afraid to eat anything in case there was a candid shot of her stuffing a meaty appetizer in her mouth.

"Zack, good to see you here."

"Jamison." Zack nodded.

"And who is this beauty?"

Naomi felt Zack's arm tense under the jacket. Despite

the pleasantries, she could practically feel Zack's strong dislike for the man grinning in front them.

"Naomi, meet my business associate, Tom Jamison."

"More like partner, my dear."

Now that wasn't what she'd expected to hear. How did Zack wind up with a partner who caused such a reaction? "Hello."

"All my pleasure." He kissed her hand, which she promptly slid out of his warm grasp.

Jamison turned to Zack. "We have to talk. I've scheduled a meeting with a few of the council members. They're really interested in our plans. If we talk to them, they'll be our biggest supporters."

"But I'm not in agreement with the plans. I said it once and I'll say it again. Might not be a good idea to have us talk to the council members."

"Do you know how much I've put on the table to make this meeting happen?"

"That could have been avoided if you'd stuck to the original plan. Instead you bring your friend into the mix without consulting me." Zack seethed. He turned his attention to Naomi. "Naomi, could you excuse me? Why don't you go chat with my mom over there."

Zack waited until Naomi hesitatingly left his side before he returned his attention and fury to Jamison. "Do you really want to have this discussion here?"

"Yes. We can take it outside to get away from this noise parading as music. Zack, there are millions of dollars at stake. I wondered why I haven't been able to reach you. Now I see what has held your undivided attention, but business still has to be conducted. We're running out of time." Jamison flashed his hands as if he were a conductor. Rings and a gaudy watch decorated his fingers and wrist. The ensemble went with the odd blue suit that made him look like an aggressive time-share seller.

Zack headed for the door with Jamison in tow. He chose the far side of the property where only a few people were out smoking. Plus, he didn't want any nosy reporters or colleagues picking up the scent of a conflict.

Jamison lit a cigarette and inhaled until it was burned halfway down. "Okay, this doesn't have to turn into World War III. I want Lassiter on board. If he's in place, we can go after the permit for the complex."

"But that's riskier. More money has to be tied up, and we have other projects. Plus, I don't think the city needs another mega-mart complex. Look around you, there are tons of empty strip malls."

"So now you're into city planning?" Jamison stepped in closer, his eyebrows meshed into one. The frown firmly in place highlighted the cold seriousness in his eyes. "Yes or no?"

"No." Zack stared back. He didn't expect any of his projects to go smoothly. The last thing he wanted was a rift, but he wasn't about to sell his soul for success.

"Then we need to discuss our next steps."

"I suggest we take the weekend to sleep on things and meet in the office on Monday."

Jamison gave a curt nod and spun on his heels. Zack watched his retreat with his posture rigid. But he wasn't the only one who was upset. He didn't know what this meant for his future business.

He headed back into the building. With an effort he shook off the residual anger. He scanned the room looking for Naomi. An apology was certainly needed, since he'd so abruptly parted with her company. His parents were on the dance floor, while Naomi was seated at a table watching them.

In an exaggerated, deep drawl, he asked, "May I interest you in a dance?" He eased closer to her, staying behind just enough that she couldn't see him.

"Oh, I don't think so. Thanks for asking. I'm waiting for the man who I came with. Sorry."

He liked the fact that she didn't bounce out of the chair for any guy. He cleared his throat to get her attention.

Before he had time to tease her, someone grabbed him by the elbow and spun him. Oh, no, it was one of the Patterson twins. Lavinia had to be one of the most tenacious women he'd ever met. Her over-the-top exuberance had turned him off then and it most certainly wasn't appropriate now. His mother referred to her and her sister as the country-club twins. His exaggerated exploits with them had now gained legendary status.

"Let's dance, Zack. Like old times." Lavinia tiptoed to look over his shoulder. "I'll bring him back when I'm done, sweetie. We've got unfinished business."

Zack followed Lavinia to the dance floor. He knew better than to call attention to her. The woman lived to be melodramatic and the source of tawdry gossip.

To make matters worse, Lavinia, clearly under the influence, promptly glued her body against his. She ground against his hips with more sultry moves than needed for the song or for him. Zack took a step back and pulled her arms from around his neck.

"I think you need to slow down on the alcohol."

"Why did you leave, Zack?" Lavinia blinked as if it helped clear her thoughts. "We were having fun. I would have settled down…with you."

"Lavinia, we were not a couple. We hung out. In a group."

"You like my sister more than me. Everyone likes her more than me." Lavinia's arms swung out in wide circles, causing him to duck.

"Are you here alone?" He'd had enough. He wasn't going to be able to get through to her while she was in this state. When she was sober, for a short window of time, she'd be embarrassed over her behavior, only to repeat the cycle.

Their group had been made up of former high school friends who went to college together. Now everyone had grown up and moved on. Lavinia couldn't quite get to that place. He'd tried to help without getting sucked into her fantasies.

"I came with someone." Lavinia looked around the room, swaying and she reached out for his hand to steady herself. "Maybe he left," she muttered.

"I'll call you a cab to take you home, okay?"

She nodded. Her mood swing had now settled to a low. "Mom will be up waiting."

Zack felt sorry for the twins' mother, who was always there to catch her daughters and sweep up the mess. He slipped his arm around her waist and led her off the dance floor to the lounge area, which wasn't private but had fewer onlookers. Quickly he made the necessary phone call and arrangements. He didn't leave her side until she was in the cab.

With Lavinia taken care of, he hurried back into the reception. Naomi was still seated at the table. As he approached, he noticed her erect posture, stiff and disapproving as she looked up at him.

He leaned in for her ears only. "If you don't mind, I

think we should go." He noted how she'd moved away from him.

She nodded but didn't take up his attempt to assist her.

Zack remained quiet, not sure what part of the night he needed to defend. So much had gone wrong. Yet he looked forward to getting out of the harsh lights and equally harsh company.

"I'll meet you out front. I need to powder my nose."

Zack nodded. The chill between him and Naomi could keep an iceberg frozen. He'd seen her keen gaze on him when Lavinia draped herself over his body. She didn't have to worry about his intentions.

"Zack, why was that cheap floozy all over you?" His mother smacked his arm. "Do you think that was appropriate behavior? What about Naomi?"

"*What about Naomi,* Mom?" He was still angry over his meeting with Jamison. His mother's scolding was like salt in a gaping wound.

"Don't make me pop you upside your head. I thought you learned better manners than that from your father. Paul, is this what you did?"

"Zack," Paul Keathley interrupted and led Zack away from his mother.

"Dad, don't start," Zack said wearily.

His father waved his hand impatiently. "Look, I'm hearing some rumblings among the council members. Frankly, it doesn't sound good."

"Like what?" Zack's stomach clenched.

"The plan is to audit your proposal and determine whether you can come through on the project. Something I need to know?"

"No. I can handle this." Zack raised his hands to

reinstate the boundaries. "Tell Mom I'm taking Naomi home."

"Let's talk tomorrow."

"Sure," Zack tossed out over his shoulder.

Naomi tapped her foot. She'd already examined her nails, looked in her pocketbook for a nonexistent thing and resisted the urge to run out of the building to catch a cab. The evening had started off on such a bright note but spiraled into something out of control. Mainly, Zack had pushed her out of his life when it proved inconvenient. She'd listened to Chantelle's stories about her brother's outrageous love life. He was like the bad boy of the Northwest region. Apparently, some women came back for more.

"Sorry to keep you waiting. My father wanted to talk to me."

"I'm ready." She walked beside Zack waiting for their car to be brought to them.

"Are you feeling cold?"

Naomi stopped rubbing her arms. She shook her head.

As soon as the car pulled up, she jumped into the passenger seat before he could help. Remembering his complaint about clingy women, she was darn sure not going to present herself like that to him.

After all, they'd had a great time, but no discussion about what was to come next. As soon as she left Seattle to return home, she'd be spending hours in the gym and with her trainer. Her body had taken a beating, but that couldn't stop her. She had to be in tip-top shape before the next season. In between the hectic schedule, where could she insert her personal life? Always looking at the practical side of things, she had to face the fact that she'd be returning to her life. The life of a professional athlete wasn't friendly toward settling down and having a family, especially when the distance between the couple was the biggest obstacle.

"We're here." Zack looked over at her.

"Thank you for the evening." She did like being in his company, even though she was unceremoniously pushed aside.

He leaned over and kissed her roughly.

She puckered for his mouth. The touch of his lips was like quenching a thirst. Though she relished his mouth covering hers, she pushed him back when his desire grew.

Naomi undid the seat belt and opened the door. "There are so many questions to ask. I have tons of thoughts rolling through. The situation doesn't get better since our emotions are running pretty high."

"What do you mean?"

"You're angry. You're kissing me with all of that emotion. I don't like being used."

Zack banged his hand against the steering wheel. "My apologies."

"What has made you so upset this evening? Your mood turned south after you introduced me to that guy Jamison."

"That's just business."

Naomi waited for a better explanation. She took in all the signs of him withdrawing—again. "Maybe it would help to talk about it."

"No. I'm fine."

Naomi pulled back. Her temper spiked. "I am good for more than one thing," she said with as much emphasis as possible.

"And I said that I was fine. Nothing to discuss or share." He stared straight ahead.

Naomi looked down at her dress. She'd wanted Zack to be impressed. Their recent past colored her thoughts about where they could go. But the cold anger that emanated from Zack evaporated such thoughts only to be replaced with doubts. She opened the car door and then twisted her body to get out before she looked over her shoulder. "All these people are around you, yet you act like you're the only one in the game. Maybe I should have gotten the rules earlier."

"Naomi—"

"Don't bother to say anything. Good night." Naomi didn't want to hear any apologies, nor did she want to hear him talk around the issue. Besides, she wasn't here to change anyone.

Chapter 8

"How are you doing?" Reba took a seat in a nearby chair while Naomi remained perched on the steps of the deck. "You look like you're pondering the world's problems."

Naomi looked down at her feet where the newspaper had fallen.

"I see you read the headlines. I don't know why Mrs. Keathley buys that local newspaper. It's no better than a gossip magazine."

The front page of the magazine was in color. The oversize title shouted out the sordid message: The Bachelor of the Year Has His Pick. As if that wasn't bad enough, the clear photo of Zack was underscored with two photos. One photo showed Zack in a tight embrace with the drunken woman at the event, while the second showed Naomi smiling at whatever he said.

Inside sources claimed that the other woman wanted

to heal their past wounds and begged for another chance. Naomi didn't necessarily believe any of the tabloid, except that she hated being portrayed as a party girl looking to have a good time. The photo of her was when they'd first arrived, full of smiles and relaxed with each other.

"Zack isn't the guy they are trying to portray."

Naomi shrugged.

"That boy is like my son. Don't you dare think that he's playing you."

"What do you want me to say, Reba?"

"That you're not letting this nonsense destroy what you have."

"Now that's the problem. Everyone thinks we have something between us. I'll be leaving here shortly. There is nothing happening between us." She said the last sentence with more emphasis. All night she'd lain awake thinking over everything Zack had told her. Maybe he didn't want this to blow up in his face. Maybe she wasn't supposed to care. She gritted her teeth against the overwhelming emotion.

Falling in love hurt like hell. Oh, man. Not cool at all.

"Your mouth is saying one thing, but I'm hearing differently. I'm a woman who's outlived two husbands and closed the chapter on one."

"That's not exactly making me feel better." Naomi had to laugh at Reba's matter-of-fact confession.

"All I'm saying is, don't jump to conclusions. If you were really interested in leaving, you'd have been gone when your grandmother left. These people are good people. There's nothing to be afraid of."

"I'm usually the one who doles out advice to my sorority sisters. I push them to fulfill their dreams or even to get their guy. I can see the problems barreling toward them at high speed. So I run interference and minimize damage. Kind of how I went headlong into the war zone with Chantelle. Why can't I do the same for myself?"

"You're looking for something that isn't there."

The chair squeaked, causing Naomi to look up. Reba came and stood near her and stroked her hair.

Her cell phone rang, interrupting any further counseling from Reba. She looked at the highlighted number. Her coach was calling. With everything that was going on, all the choices that she needed to consider, having a conversation with her coach had the potential to force a decision.

"I'll leave you alone. I'm making a big pot of chicken noodle soup." Reba stepped back into the house while she answered.

"Thanks, Reba." Naomi pressed the button to talk to her coach. "Hi, Coach Brewster."

"Naomi! My gosh, I've been worried about you."

"Sorry, Coach. I meant to call you after my doctor's visit yesterday. I'm healing well."

"I know. I got a full report. All good news. Couldn't be more pleased." Her coach paused, her silence full of expectancy. "I know you are offline for a while. Didn't expect you still to be in Washington."

"Me either. I decided to make it a vacation."

"Smart move. Everything else fine?"

Naomi closed her eyes. She cleared her throat and pasted a bright smile on her face. "Everything is fantastic. Just laying low, you know what I mean."

"Right. Right. Well, I got a strange call from a photographer."

"I don't understand."

"A photographer from Washington wants to speak to

you. Don't really know why they came to me. You're right there, aren't you? Or did you leave and not tell me?"

"I just said that I went to the doctor. Did the photographer say who they worked for?" Naomi glanced down at the newspaper and flipped it over. She'd rather look at the local supermarket specials for the week than at Zack and that other woman glued to each other.

"Mentioned a modeling agency. I barely understood him. The guy had a strong European accent. Do you want me to send him to your agent?"

"Um…no, I'll take the information." Naomi wasn't fooled by the modeling ruse. This had to be a nosy reporter pushing into her life to get more information. She grabbed the newspaper and crushed it in her grasp. Well, she was ready for this worm.

"Okay. Here's the number." Her coach read off the number and other identifying information. "Keep in touch."

Naomi hung up and then stared at the number. She would call the number but would wait. She wasn't in the frame of mind to have a civil conversation. Plus, there really wasn't any reason to give her side of anything. Modeling, indeed; she was a tomboy who could occasionally get dressed up. The reporter needed to come up with something a little more original.

Zack stared at the phone on his desk. He'd wanted to call Naomi so many times but had resisted the urge. Calling her required something from him. He'd have to explain and give details about his thoughts, even his fears. Right now, he barely had a handle on what was going on in his mind.

"Zack." His secretary popped in her head through the open door. "Your father is here to see you."

Zack straightened his tie and smoothed the front of his shirt. He'd just adjusted himself in the chair when his father entered his office.

A visit from his father wasn't frequent, and more specifically it wasn't unannounced. From his father's serious expression, this visit wasn't a fun drop-in.

"I've been trying to reach you all night, especially after you dropped off Naomi."

"I had a lot on my mind. I wasn't answering the phone."

"That's why I came to you." His father took a seat. "Look, I'm not liking what I'm hearing out there. I'm trying to get to the bottom of it. But at the moment, I'm more concerned that your company is coming under scrutiny."

"This is what you were talking about last night?"

His father nodded.

"I haven't heard anything."

"Instead of waiting for the hammer to fall, why don't we set up a meeting with the council members? Let's find out what the issues are and then we can fix them before the entire council gets together to vote or take action."

"Dad, I think you're thinking the worst of the situation. Like I said, no one has informed me of any scrutiny. And besides, I want to be able to handle this."

"On your own?" His father shook his head. "This isn't the time to be stubborn. Look, I'm proud of where you've gotten with your company. But we can combine forces and be pretty formidable. This is your legacy."

"I appreciate what you're saying. This company wasn't created to get under your skin. You focus on residential and I focus on commercial. I want a chance to make mistakes, take risks, follow my strategy. You taught me all those things. Now I want to put them to good use," Zack argued.

"I get it, but this is important. Why be stubborn? You don't have to prove yourself to me. Your mother. Any one."

Zack groaned and pushed back from the desk. On the surface, his father would think that he was being rebellious. There was that side to him. A side that showed itself more so when he was a teenager.

After college, returning home as an adult, he didn't have it in him to be a pain. Instead he wanted his father's approval.

His phone rang, but he allowed his assistant to receive the call. Less than a minute later, he bade her enter.

"Zack, it's Councilman Wayans."

"I'll take it."

"Don't commit to anything." His father leaned forward.

Zack nodded. His pulse shot up. A certain queasiness flooded his stomach. His father's forecast had turned into reality.

"Hello, Councilman. What can I do for you?"

"Zack, good to see you last night. I wished that we'd had time to talk, though. Looks like you had lots of people vying for your attention."

"I always have time for you, Councilman." Zack forced himself to stay quiet. He didn't want to play this social game any longer.

"I want to give you a heads-up that an investigation is being conducted on the proposal process and on who won. That would be your company."

"Should I be concerned?" The question could have been rhetorical. His nerves were on high alert.

"No, not at all. I'm sure all will be in order. Just means that we'll be delayed with a final decision."

"When will this audit begin?"

"Immediately."

"I can't help but feel that this is directed at my company."

"No, not at all. We have a very active citizen watchdog group and they asked for the audit. With reelections pending, well, they were heard."

Zack had also met with the watchdog group. He had assuaged many of their concerns. Now he had to wonder what had stirred them up enough to request an audit.

"Zack, believe me, this is not unusual. You'll get the formal letter either today or tomorrow. If you have any questions, feel free to call me."

"Thanks, Councilman." Zack hung up the phone slowly. He was already thinking ahead, wondering how to proceed. Despite the disagreement with Jamison, he still had to inform him of this latest development. And then there was his father.

"Son, don't underestimate what is happening." He rose, his age showing in the slow movement and the way he winced. "My help is always here if you want it."

Zack nodded.

"Oh, by the way, your mother expects you home for dinner. The local paper has you and Naomi as the front-cover stars."

Zack groaned, this time holding his head. He'd no idea that Naomi was now the target of the paper.

"See you later." His father waved.

Zack looked at his watch. He had a few more calls to make before a meeting. Dinner at his mother's was definitely a mandatory appearance.

* * *

Naomi drove into town. She appreciated Francis lending her the car. She wanted to get out of the house and the thoughts that raised too many questions.

After wandering through the mall, Naomi drove through the various neighborhoods. Seattle was a picturesque city with so much lush greenery, hilly streets, and the businesses and restaurants along Puget Sound and Lake Washington.

Her solitary meandering made her miss her friends terribly. She missed the sorority life that had brought them close in college. After graduation, her sorors were able to attend the chapter meetings and go to events, but her schedule prevented her from participating.

Instead of getting closer as they got older, they were creating their separate paths. Naomi missed those days and evenings where she could throw herself across their beds and listen to their problems and share advice. Although she'd made friends with her teammates, they didn't replace the special bond she shared with her sorors.

Naomi hit the ATM for some cash. Maybe she'd pop into a movie and while away the afternoon. Sitting in the darkened theater with a spattering of other viewers would add to the loneliness. She pulled out her phone. Why act as if she was on another planet? She began to text when her phone vibrated with an incoming text from Denise. When R U cmng bck

Then from Sara. Have u fallen off the face of earth

Then Asia. Whoz the man that has u tied up

Naomi giggled. They obviously had planned an intervention.

The constant incoming texts interrupted a few of the

patrons sitting nearby. Their muttering complaints grew louder. Naomi didn't care about the movie and hastily left.

Then Athena's message vibrated. Ur grndmom sez u have boyfriend. Last 2 no.

Naomi waited. One of them would hook them all up on a conference call. A minute later, her phone rang. She hurried to her car where she could laugh and talk or more like scream over the equally exuberant chatter of her sorority sisters.

"Hello, sorors." Already, Naomi felt better.

The chorus of greetings made her giggle and ushered in a warmth where the cold ache of missing her friends had settled. She breezed through their opening questions about her health and the Keathleys.

"Okay, enough," Athena interrupted her detailed description of Frannie's garden. "Who is Zack? I want details as if you were describing the flowers and herbs and all that crap." Athena complained that she'd have to get back to work.

Naomi sighed. "Guess it's my turn for the third degree."

"And about time, I might add." Athena's twin, Asia, interrupted.

"You know the actor Idris Elba?" Naomi cut to the chase.

"No." Sara was usually clueless about movie stars unless she saw their photo.

"He looks like that?" Denise's voice grew excited.

"Yes, and then some." Naomi chuckled. "Check out his Web site, you'll see a very handsome photo."

"Is that why you're still there?" Sara asked.

"No, I'm actually recuperating." Naomi hadn't told

them the details of the assault. She knew her sorors, and their attention would be overwhelming.

"I think you can recuperate here in Chicago where we can spoil you even more rotten than you already are," Sara offered.

"Wait a minute!" Athena interrupted. "Are you relocating? You cannot copy me."

"I'm not relocating. I do have a career."

"Well, that's low. I was laid off." Asia argued.

"And before I get pulled into this, I took a legitimate job. Overseas," Athena piped up.

"So when are you coming back home, Naomi?" Sara pushed.

"Well…" Naomi paused. When was she coming back? After reading the newspaper, she'd been prepared to pack her suitcase. Now, talking to her sorors, she realized that she was not the type to run away. Only one thing could send her on her way, and that was Zack. Even if he said those words, she'd stubbornly do the opposite.

"She's not done playing with her new toy," Denise explained, a sense of realization creeping into her voice.

"Something like that." Naomi's new attitude gave her some spunk.

"I want to be there," Denise whined.

"I'll be back soon. Reality is knocking. Got to get back to work." Asia complained.

Athena piped up. "Okay, soror. Answer your e-mails too. And send a picture or two."

Naomi wished every one of them well. Funny how life turned out. They'd graduated together from university and were now scattered all over living grown-up lives with husbands, significant others and children.

According to her sorors, she was the last holdout. Although Zack was in her life, and she faced the reality of being in love, she wasn't one to rely on pure emotion to keep any man.

However, she had something to do. She placed another call to the house before starting her borrowed car and heading for the next destination.

By the time she pulled into the parking lot housing KBD Corporation, she wasn't too sure about her gutsy move.

"Naomi?"

Naomi jumped. A sharp knock on the driver's-side window startled her. She opened the window. "Hi, Zack."

"What are you doing here?"

"Nice to see you, too," she answered wryly.

"Sorry." He opened the door for her to exit. "You caught me by surprise."

"Are you heading out?"

"I was going to lunch. I'm supposed to come over for dinner."

"That's probably for my benefit. I guess you haven't had to eat at home as much as since I arrived." She grinned.

"How precise you are."

"Are you flying solo for lunch?" She tossed out the question as if the answer didn't matter. Yet her breath held in case it was the buxom Miss Pacific Northwest from the tabloids. "I'm here to take you to lunch."

Surprise registered on Zack's face, but he was polite enough to erase it. "I'd love to go."

"Hop in, you can point me in the right direction."

Zack walked around the front of the car and got in. He slipped on his seat belt and then sat back with his hands firmly planted on his legs. "Looks like you're in the driver's seat."

"As much as possible when it comes to my life."

"What cuisine are you interested in eating?"

"Doesn't matter. Something I can pronounce, though."

"Okay. There's a great seafood place about five miles up the coast." Zack directed her to the location.

Naomi followed the directions, noting that Zack kept busy texting. She didn't complain; after all, she had busted into his day. He probably had lots of appointments that he had to reschedule, even though he said he was free. Although she felt bad, she didn't feel guilty enough to change her mission.

The drive along the coastline served to calm her nerves a bit. Expensive real estate lined the shore with the occasional restaurant. The view of the parking lot with the expensive cars was a sign that the establishments catered to the higher income.

Dressed in jeanslike leggings and a minidress, she figured that she could enter any restaurant without problems. Luckily, Zack wore a suit.

"At the next intersection, turn left."

"Left?" Naomi looked in the direction but clearly didn't see any restaurants.

"Yes."

Naomi noted the small smile that lifted the corner of Zack's mouth. What was he up to? But she was game. She turned left and headed down the street.

Doubts didn't cease. As a matter of fact, she slowed at the sight of the marina that housed a large array of yachts and boats.

"Park over there." Zack pointed off to the right.

Naomi didn't bother to question it, since she was curious. She parked and turned off the engine.

"I'd say that now you must switch drivers. It's my turn to do the driving."

"Really?" She got out the car and followed him down the pier to a midsize yacht. "I thought that we were going to a seafood restaurant."

"Actually, I only promised that you'd have seafood for lunch. As for the place, step on board." Zack moved aside for her to walk up the plank.

A uniformed attendant met her at the opening. "Welcome, Miss Venable."

"Hi." Naomi looked at Zack for an explanation.

"Thanks, Gus. Miss Venable and I will start with a light appetizer."

"Yes, sir."

"Okay, who was that? Is this yours? How did you know that I would come here? How did you do all this?" Naomi walked ahead of Zack. The spread of white tablecloth with fresh flowers and wineglasses pulled her attention. She turned to shoot more questions, but the sound of the yacht's engines firing up distracted her.

She hurried to the rail and looked down at the water churning furiously. The land retreated at a fast rate as they headed out toward deeper waters.

She shook her head, wondering if she could ever stay one step ahead of him. Zack continually amazed her.

Chapter 9

"You look petrified." Zack slipped his hand around her shoulders. "Here's a glass of wine."

"Only one. I do have to take you back to your office."

"Yes, you do. And I do have a troubling matter to deal with."

"Care to share?"

"Just business."

"See, that's what brought me to your office in the first place." Naomi set down her glass. Some wine splashed over the rim.

"What do you mean?"

She sighed. A sound that held sadness and disappointment. Zack knew he was the source. The witty banter died.

"Talk to me, Naomi. What's bothering you?"

"It's more like what's not bothering you." She looked

him square in the eye. "We met, became friends, got intimate, but then you won't share details about your business, your company. It's an important part of your life."

"I tend not to share details about my company."

"Yeah, you've made that clear."

"Excuse me, Mr. Keathley, your appetizer." Gus, the waiter, set down two small bowls of soup.

Zack waited for Naomi to test hers with a dainty sip from the spoon. Despite her irritation with him, he couldn't resist the smile after she tasted the bisque.

"I'll eat. You talk." She pointed at him with the spoon.

Nothing about his life was top secret. But he also never shared too many intimate details with any of his female friends. Deep down he knew they wouldn't last beyond a date or two. No need to pretend that a lasting relationship existed.

Things had changed, tossed on their ear, when he walked into the hospital room that day. Naomi, injured and medicated, had wrapped him around her little finger.

"I'm almost done." She looked down at her bowl.

Zack looked longingly at his bowl but knew better than to reach for it. Maybe it was the way she waved the spoon, as if it could suddenly turn into a weapon.

"I always had the dream to step out on my own. Have my own business. Move out of my father's shadow." He paused. "As I tell you my history, it sounds so much like my father's." Zack shook his head. His reality was a bit ironic. "The Keathleys are in the land-development business. I was so determined not to be shoehorned into the family empire that I did everything in my power to push aside my father. Starting the business with this partner was one way to untangle any ties."

"Sounds like you had good intentions."

"Naive ones." He sighed. "There is so much politicking behind the scenes, blatant greed mentality and just bad luck that I wonder if I should throw in the towel. Problem is that I love what I do. Now I've got the city council out of the blue pushing for all kinds of documentation and wanting to audit. Then one project may not go through because the anchor business wants to flex its muscle. On another project, my partner wants to renege on the conditions. Plus he wanted to increase his partnership share. Not going to happen." He growled.

In an abbreviated manner, he shared the basic information about his company and partners. Then he moved onto the steady deterioration of the biggest project in his portfolio with the impending audit by the city council.

"Here." Naomi offered him his bowl.

He waited for her response, but she only nudged her chin at him. Taking the hint, he started drinking his soup.

"Why was that such a big deal?"

"It's my company. My problems."

"In other words, you're a control freak," she proclaimed. "A blind optimist and a dreamer." She leaned over and kissed him on his cheek. "I like these qualities in a man."

He turned to take full advantage of her mouth. Spilling the soup didn't matter.

But she pulled away, wagging her finger. "No. no. Not so fast. I want to know one more thing."

"I told you everything."

"Why shouldn't I continue to pack my suitcase and head back to Chicago?"

"Were you packing?" Zack sat up. He waved Gus away, not wanting any distractions. "I don't want you to leave."

"I'm not ready to leave. But I have to know that you're willing to step up and not build your wall between us."

"It's been on my mind. I like having you here, but I don't want you to ever think that I'm asking you to make a decision between your career and me."

"You may not have to."

A small change in Naomi's demeanor alerted him that there was more to the statement. Should he hope? He took her hand, looking down at her palm as if it could provide the answers he sought. Her hand closed around his. He glanced at the gold-tone nail polish on her elegant fingers. "Let's eat."

Gus magically appeared with covered plates. With a small flourish, he whipped open the covers. Perfectly grilled tilapia surrounded by a colorful array of vegetables and small russet potatoes completed the meal. Zack was hungry, but he preferred to watch Naomi inhale the succulent scent and look at him with an appreciative smile.

"You certainly know how to woo a woman."

"I love the way you chew."

"That sexy talk will get you somewhere," she laughed. They ate and talked until it was mid-afternoon. "I think you need to get back to work."

"I hate not being able to spend the day with you."

"I'll be busy," she hinted.

"Are you going to share?"

"Nope. I'm not certain yet."

Zack raised his hand in the air and motioned for Gus to slow the yacht and turn. Every second he was with Naomi he hated having the return to reality, especially when it didn't include her presence.

"You came out here to set me straight." Zack accompanied Naomi to stand at the rail. "So was the mission accomplished?"

Naomi closed the gap and placed her hands around his waist. She stared into his eyes. He felt as if they were syncing without words but through pure emotions. Her desire washed over him, bathing him in a warm cocoon of sensuality. He tried to wait for her to make the first move. But he couldn't wait any longer.

"Kiss me," she ordered.

"Shh."

"Don't shush—"

Zack pulled Naomi against his body. Her firm body against his had already caused a physical reaction. Under the salty wind lightly swirling around them, he kissed Naomi like a man reaching out for a water bottle in a desert. Straight up, nothing compared to tasting and savoring her.

His hands slid up her back and he pinned her in his embrace. He couldn't stop kissing her, playing with her willing tongue in a game of moves that stirred every part of him.

"Save some for later," she mumbled against his mouth.

"Only because Gus is onboard." Zack closed his eyes tightly as he pressed his cheek next to Naomi's. He had to bring his body under control so he could sound like a sane man.

Naomi kissed his neck. "Good. We're on the same page."

"Don't do that." He flinched. "You need to stand over there and keep your hands on the railing."

"But I'd much rather have my hands do this." Her hand trailed up his inner thigh stopping short at his zipper. Restraining her hand didn't matter. Or he didn't try hard enough to deter her from her exploratory search.

"You like to play dangerously."

"That's why I often earn the MVP award."

"You'll hear no arguments from me."

Zack waited until Naomi pulled out of the parking lot before heading into his office. Spending the lunch hour with Naomi had re-energized his system. Although the audit would be a pain, he refused to just let the project slip through his fingers.

"Rachel, get Jamison on the phone. I need to talk to him, as soon as possible."

"Yes, sir. You look quite determined. Your lunch must have done you good."

"In more ways than one." He went to his office and waited for a sign that the call awaited his attention.

His secretary popped in her head. "Sorry, he's out of the office. I left a message. Didn't leave any further details, since I don't know what you wanted with him."

He could hear the accusation. "No need to be worried. I took the lunch break to think about my options."

"Hope you got some good thinking done and didn't get distracted by a celeb on rehab."

"That sounded very judgmental. Not wanted."

"Sorry." Rachel, his assistant from day one of his business sometimes acted as if she ran his life. He made sure to keep the relationship completely professional.

Zack turned his attention back to his desk. He had two properties to visit, but he'd wait until tomorrow, since they would take him to the other side of town. One glance at the clock showed that he had two hours before the mandatory appearance at his mother's table.

A knock interrupted him. He looked up slightly irritated by the interruption. "Zack, your father and Brent are here to see you."

"What?" Zack looked down at the papers, wondering why his father needed to see him. They had already spoken. His buddy was also with his father, which had to be coincidental. The timing sucked, though.

"Where do you want to talk? In your office or the board-room?"

"I'll see them here. I'll talk to my father first."

"Okay, but they came into the office together."

Zack tossed down the pen he held. His father had left this morning now only to return and with his friend, the very person he was about to turn to for help with finding his birth mother. He fought to look cool under his father's scrutiny.

His father led the way into his office. He took a seat on the couch. His friend, however, came over and gave him a bear hug. His ex-football physique had barely diminished since college. Zack hated playing flag football against him on campus. Inevitably Brent forgot that he didn't have to tackle but simply pull off the flag on his opponent.

"I was hoping you were on this coast," Zack finally said after being released from Brent's grasp.

"I'm only here for a short bit. I've got some business to wrap up and then I'll be heading back to the East Coast. Nothing like spending winter in Boston."

"It's not like you couldn't afford to have a place in Miami, now that you're the man."

"I must have missed the big news. Aren't you a lawyer?" Zack's father asked.

"I left that life to create a sports and entertainment agency."

"You know the college kid who was just drafted to the L.A. basketball team?" Zack pointed toward Brent. "And you know the pop star that dresses in those crazy outfits?"

"You mean the one that barely has on any clothes?" Paul responded. "Her mother needs to slap her upside her head."

"Well, that's Brent, too."

"Son, I'm proud of you. Good to see that you've made a success out of all the hard work and money that you've put in."

"Thanks, sir. Couldn't have done it without my parents, though. Pops, may he rest in peace, sacrificed a lot to make sure I got into college and stayed there. I was glad that he got to see the agency start before he passed."

"Your father was a good man." Zack's father shook his head. "How's your mother? And your sisters?"

"Mom is doing fine. She's living with Evelyn in Georgia. My other two sisters are sharing an apartment in New York while they're both finishing up college. I'll let them know that I got a chance to see you."

"Please do. I am glad that I thought of calling you to see what you could do for Zack."

"What's going on, Zack? How can I help? Your father filled me in on the issues you're having with your business partners."

Zack glared at his father, who seemed oblivious to his emotion.

"Hey, bro, let me see if I can help you."

"I'm not worried about the city council, but I'm getting bad vibes from this man and a partner who suddenly stepped into the picture."

"What's the guy's name?"

"Seth Lassiter. My associate is Tom Jamison."

Brent's eyebrows shot up. He whistled.

"What?" Zack and his father asked.

"I've heard of the guy. Not all good. He's not from this area, which means that he wants to move in. But he probably can't do so under his own name. He's a shark in the land-development business. Nothing illegal, just on the edge, and pretty cutthroat with his methods."

"So in other words, Zack needs to stay away from him?"

"Stay away from him and his partner. I'm sure the problem now is how to get rid of the partner. I would've loved the chance to take them down in the legal arena."

"Exactly." Zack couldn't believe the hole that he'd gotten himself into. This was a fairly simple deal that would revitalize the neighborhood. Now he was about to step in the mud with a couple of crabs.

"Let me look at your contract. I'll get back to you as soon as I can. I do have to leave in a couple of days, but I don't have to be here to assist you. I've got your back."

"Thanks, Brent. I'll wait to hear from you before I head to a lawyer." Zack promptly sent an e-mail to Rachel letting her know to gather the information that Brent would need.

"What are you doing this evening, Brent?" Zack's father asked.

"Um…I may have a mixer to attend. But Zack, I'd love to have you come. You never know, you might get lucky."

"Sounds like fun, but I can't." Zack preferred to keep Naomi out of the spotlight.

"Brent, before you head out for a night of fun, you've got to come to the house. Frannie would be happy to see you. And you could also meet Naomi Venable. She's recuperating after an assault over two weeks ago. I think Zack—fancies her."

"Zack fancies her," Brent teased. "Hmm…now that might be something I'd like to see. Count me in. What time is dinner?" Brent grinned at Zack.

Zack's father happily filled in the details as they walked out of his office. Zack remained seated, since neither one had really paid him any attention. Naomi was the topic of conversation.

He didn't mind introducing her to Brent. He'd already let her in about his company, his life, and now one of his dear friendships. The door kept getting wider and wider, even as he kept a firm grip on the handle in case he needed to shut it.

He took a deep breath and exhaled. He had to admit that he felt better that Brent was checking into the problems. Now he could head home and face a different kind of drama, created by his mother.

Dinner turned into a festive occasion. Zack watched the delight on his mother's face as she fawned over Brent and laughed over his compliments. His father's face beamed with pride over Brent's recounts of their friendship in college and afterward. Brent had become one of the family during that time when he stayed with him over the summer holidays. Even Reba seemed to fall under his best friend's spell. He observed that Naomi also jumped into the conversation but didn't appear as gushing as his parents. He felt strangely glad about that.

After dinner they sat in the living room with a small fire burning in the fireplace. His parents had already excused themselves so the young people could have a chance to talk. Zack refilled Brent's glass with iced tea.

"Naomi, here's my business card. I'm not going to wait for Zack to tell you that I'm in the sports and entertainment arena." Brent handed her a card.

"Thank you. Zack tends to be shy about his personal business."

"I don't know why. If you need to know anything, just ask me. I'd be happy to volunteer information," Brent whispered in a loud, husky voice.

"Think he's sincere?"

Zack almost choked on his drink. He looked at Naomi, who had her full attention on Brent. He shifted his gaze to Brent, hoping that his friend would give him the courtesy of looking at him. He felt like the proverbial fly on the wall.

"Zack is a pretty sincere guy. He's shut down over the years—heartbreak and rejection does that."

"Oh, is he still moping over a heartbreak?" Naomi teased.

"He shouldn't be. He lost her to me in our junior year in college. She saw me make the winning touchdown and decided that she didn't want to be with the college cheerleader when she could be with the star player."

"I could let all the other bs fly, but I'm not admitting to being a cheerleader."

"Personally, I think you would have made a cute cheerleader." Naomi wrinkled her nose at him.

"Don't you start."

"Zack was a lacrosse player," Brent clarified.

"Lacrosse? I'm impressed."

"What about me? Football." Brent curled his forearm popping his bicep into an impressive muscled hump.

Naomi made a face. "I like a touch of the unique and exotic."

Zack grinned.

"I tried." Brent shrugged. "Tell me about basketball and you."

"Stop shopping for new clients."

"No, it's okay. Actually, I got a call from a photographer interested in talking to me about modeling."

"Did you call him back?"

"No, I was trying to decide if that's what I wanted to do."

"And?" Zack thought she could be a fantastic model, but he didn't want to push.

"Lady, with your height, good looks and fantastic body…" Brent raised his hands in mock surrender. "Not that I'm checking you out, but I know you can model, act, whatever you want to do."

"And I'm sure you'd be willing to help with all of that." Zack could see the calculations regarding commissions flying over Brent's head as he added up all avenues of income.

"No joke, no kidding around, let me do the footwork. Not asking you to sign anything."

"Not yet, anyway," Zack interrupted. He trusted

his friend but didn't want him pushing Naomi into anything.

"You've got a deal." Naomi offered her hand and firmly shook Brent's hand.

"My pleasure." Brent kissed her hand.

Zack rolled his eyes. But he was glad that Naomi looked happy with her decision.

"Brent, nice meeting you. I'm going to excuse myself and allow you all to bond."

"You don't have to leave." Zack stood with her.

"I have to, otherwise how would I know what Brent really thinks about me?" Naomi laughed.

After Naomi left, he and Brent reconnected. Now that they were both busy, their lives didn't often intersect. He missed his buddy.

They chatted until the fire died, leaving only burning embers. Brent looked at his watch. "Guess I missed that mixer."

"I'm sure it's still going on."

"It's been a long day. I don't have the stamina I used to have."

"I know what you mean. That's why I've long retired from the meat-market scene at nightclubs."

"Must be easy to do now that you're with Naomi."

"It's all temporary. One day, she'll be returning home to her life."

Brent headed for the front door. Then he turned and said, "Doesn't have to be that ending. Just tell her what's on your mind."

"What's that exactly?"

"That you love her." Brent didn't wait for his response, instead closing the front door on his exit.

Chapter 10

Naomi came downstairs to the smell of a full, hearty breakfast. She identified possible waffles or pancakes, definitely bacon and eggs, but there were other items that had the wonderful mix of tomatoes, herbs and potatoes. She was getting used to these grand meals, which would be her downfall when it was time to start practice.

"I'm going to be so spoiled," she said, as she rounded the corner. "Oh." She stopped short.

"Didn't mean to startle you," Zack said. The sight of Zack standing in front to the stove stirring a pot was sexy as hell. "Where's Reba?"

"She had to go see her sister for a few days in California."

"And you came to the rescue?"

"I want you to know that I'm quite capable of providing a meal. I think that I fed you…in more than one way."

Naomi blushed.

"Have a seat and I'll serve breakfast."

"Where are your parents?"

"Probably gone for one of their morning walks together."

"Oh, yes, they do go whenever Mr. Keathley doesn't have an early morning at work."

Naomi waited until Zack was seated, but only barely. Her plate was filled with the mouthwatering food. After saying Grace, she dug in.

"I heard from Brent."

"And…?"

"Looks like my first job will be the women's lingerie in the great outdoors. I think they are looking at some locations farther north."

"That sounds pretty chilly."

"I know. Besides, revealing my body has my nerves on edge."

"Revealing your body has *my* nerves on edge."

Naomi smiled. After cleaning her plate, she reached for the small bowl of fresh fruit.

"Now that I know what you'll be doing, I may have a plan." Zack tapped his temple.

"Really? What's that?"

"I'll let it be a surprise."

Naomi shrugged to show that she wasn't excited by his mischievous glint. The way he smiled turned her stomach in a jittery mess.

"This was wonderful. Having breakfast with you." Naomi smiled at him.

"I miss you."

"You've seen me often enough."

"Yeah, but it's been a 'see but don't touch' moment."

"This is true. But it is what is. I do enjoy our meals together."

Zack tossed down his napkin with irritation. "Yeah, with my parents watching us."

"They do seem pleased with themselves."

Naomi stood and started to clear the dishes.

"I'll get those."

"Hey, it's my turn. When I get back home, there won't be anyone serving me or washing my things."

The silence dropped, heavy and intrusive. Naomi gritted her teeth at how insensitive she must have sounded. And hopefully not desperate. She noticed that Zack paused in helping to take up the dishes, but didn't say anything. Didn't ask anything.

Switching subjects, she asked, "Um…is everything straight with your partners?"

"No. I'm working on dissolving the partnership. May cost me in more than one way."

Naomi's head snapped up. "What happened?"

"Not sure yet."

"Don't do this." Naomi set down the plates on the counter. She faced him with her hands on her hips. "Don't retreat. I'm really interested in what's going on."

"One of the men that is entangled in this has a shady reputation. Pushing him out may not be nice and tidy."

"Can you pay him to leave?"

"He's not a partner, so I don't have to pay him. I do, however, have to get rid of the person who was partnering with me on this project."

"Why don't you get your father's help? He's got the reputation and clout to step in on your behalf and get these men to back off."

Zack tossed the dishcloth into the sink and uttered a disgusted grunt. Then he leaned against the sink with his shoulders hunched and head bowed.

Naomi noted that this man's pride could cripple his success.

"I can hear you call me names, even though your mouth isn't moving."

"Good." Naomi crossed her arms, glaring at his profile.

"I'll talk to him."

Naomi tapped her foot.

"Today. I'll go to my father today."

"Talk to me about what?"

Naomi jumped. She hadn't heard Zack's parents return. Zack looked equally surprised and uncomfortable, since he had no choice but to continue with the conversation.

Naomi patted Zack on the shoulder. "I'll let you two talk. I have to prepare for my new career." She left the kitchen despite Zack's protests. This conversation between father and son had to be done. She saw Zack turning to his father for help as a milestone needed to aid in the conflict that appeared to exist between them.

In the meantime, she hurried through her morning therapeutic exercise routines and then settled on her bed with laptop and pen and paper. While Zack dealt with difficult issues, she had her own challenges. She had to take her own advice and place the necessary call.

"Hi, Coach."

"Naomi, how are you? Everything okay? I'm heading down to the lobby for breakfast and then we're on the move for the final game in San Diego."

"How have things been going? Has the fan turnout been good?"

"It's been fantastic. Good to see so many young girls with mothers and even fathers come out. Many of the players have diehard fans that keep track of them online. It's all pretty cool. So many girls asked about you."

"That's sweet." Naomi missed this part of the professional business. She always looked forward to talking with her young fans. "I miss everyone."

"Is that the reason for the call?" Her coach probed. "Are you still in Seattle?"

"Yes. I'm…well, I'm going to model."

"Model?"

"I got offered a contract for a photograph layout for a sports magazine."

"I suppose wearing next to nothing." Her coach's disapproval came through loud and clear.

"Lingerie."

"Why?"

"It's time for me to look at other options."

"How about a news broadcaster, assistant coach and just a basketball player with another ten years in her?"

"You ever wanted to be the sexy girl?"

"Who says I'm not that now or never was?" Her coach chuckled.

"This is a legitimate avenue for me to pursue. I can model, endorse some items, maybe create my own things. I want more than basketball."

"I presume that your agent doesn't know you're calling me."

"Of course not, we've always dealt directly with each other and let the suits do what they have to do. Nothing has changed."

"I appreciate it, even if I don't agree."

"This project will let me know if I'm excited about

the career or just the thought of being on a magazine cover. I'll get back to you."

Her coach sighed. "Let me know what's happening."

Naomi hung up and stared at the animated screensaver on her laptop. She suspected more people than her coach would be disappointed with her choice. The one person who really mattered was the last to know. She took a deep breath seeking courage from deep within herself before placing the next call.

"Grandma? Hi, it's Naomi."

"Calling with good news, I hope."

"Good news? I think so. Did Frannie tell you?" Naomi had hoped she could break the news to her grandmother.

"All Frannie said was to let you tell me. I'm so happy and proud of you."

Naomi exhaled, trying to eliminate the nervous knots. Her grandmother's support was important. "I'll be gone for a few days next week. I'm not sure what issue it will come out."

"Gone for the engagement? I don't understand."

"Engagement?"

"To Zack."

"Frannie told you that I was getting engaged to Zack?"

"Well, no, just that you would have something to tell me. She sounded happy. I just assumed."

"It's not about Zack." Her pulse, which had spiked at the thought of Zack proposing to her, returned to normal. "I'll be modeling."

"Well, that's another big surprise."

"How do you feel?"

"Honey, I'm behind anything you want to do. If modeling is what you want to do, then I'm all for it. You are a pretty girl. Look just like your mother."

"I'll be modeling lingerie."

"And you've got the body to do it. You're a grown woman, and I'm sure you'll handle yourself with class and dignity."

"I wish you were here so I could hug you tight."

"I wish that I was with you, too."

Naomi caught up on her grandfather's health. She wanted to ask about her mother but fought the urge. She hated feeling the need to know how she was doing when her mother didn't inquire about her. But she wanted her mother to know that despite her absence, she'd done well. Her grandparents had stepped in and provided the love that she needed. Her grandmother had taught her all about being a good woman.

"Well, I'll talk to you later. Got to take your grandfather to his doctor's appointment. Don't forget to tell me all about it when you get back."

"I will. Love you." Naomi hung up with her grandmother.

Now that she'd talked to her coach and her grandmother, she felt much better. Their opinions did matter, but she still had to make up her mind. Once she'd committed to working with Brent for her new modeling career, she felt sure that she'd made the right decision.

A new challenge, a new life possibly awaited her. She ran toward it with open arms. All she wanted now was for Zack to be there in front of her, ready and waiting. She knew that she loved him. But to hear her grandmother mention engagement and all that came with it like a wedding and life happily ever after, Naomi wanted that more than ever.

However, she couldn't honestly say that Zack felt the same. She felt as if she'd only been able to penetrate the first inches of his shell. She could offer him much, but trust was something that he would have to feel and believe. Without trust, they had nothing between them. This momentary beginning to something pure and sincere couldn't live without trust.

Naomi pushed the thoughts aside. Instead she focused on where she might want the next phase of her career to go. Brent requested the information, suggesting that she needed to think, focus, write it down and then make it a reality. She'd never done anything without giving it every ounce of her effort. Going off to be a model seemed like a viable option.

"Dad, I need your help."

"You've got it." His father raised his hands. "And with no strings attached."

Zack nodded.

"It may mean that you have to give up on the project. The council will simply withdraw the permit."

"What about the audit? I don't want any stains on my reputation."

"I couldn't stop it. That would have raised a lot of questions. Don't worry about it."

"Considering that they don't audit companies that are okay, this action puts a certain stigma on my name."

"Not true. My company has been audited because of the amount of work I've done. It also happened when I was relatively new to the business. It's one of those painful exercises that must be done."

Zack nodded. "Okay, this will work."

"I'm glad Naomi encouraged you to come to me. I've been dying to help."

"I know, Dad." Zack scooted to the edge of the chair, bringing him closer to his father. "Dad, I need to tell you something else." He paused.

"Go ahead."

"I'm going to come out and say it."

"What?"

"I've been thinking about my birth mother."

His father's hand paused in midair as he was about to stroke his head. Then he lowered it, resting one hand in the other. Finally he looked up at Zack.

"I'm thinking about going to Haiti."

"Could you slow down for a second?"

Zack paused. He felt himself getting defensive. His father's knitted brow and tight-lipped expression told of his real feelings.

"Do you have information to locate your birth mother?"

"No. Not yet."

"I told you everything I knew." His father cleared his throat. "You know, I don't want you to go to your mother with this news."

"I don't think it's right to keep it from her."

"It was her one fear."

"Finding my mother?"

"Losing you."

Zack stood, opting to pace in the confines of the office. "Mom can never lose me." He chose to address that concern rather than the other topic of him going to Haiti to find his mother, maybe even his family.

"Nevertheless, I'll tell her."

"I'd love to hand over the responsibility, but I can't.

This is something that Mom and I have to discuss. You can have a separate conversation with her."

"Do you know when you're going?" his father inquired, seeming more unsettled than usual.

"I don't even know *if* I'm going. The subject has been on my mind. I wanted to let you know." How could he explain the dreams that he had? Some were bits and pieces of intense recollections as a child in his homeland. Other scenarios were of a future event when he reunited with his birth mother.

"I'll have to wrap my head around this. But I want you to know that I support you."

"Thanks, Dad."

His father hugged, then released him. Clearly his thoughts now took over and their conversation was complete. Zack took the opportunity to leave. He'd hoped his father would be more enthusiastic. Yet he understood the older man's fears. At some point, sooner rather than later, he had to tell his mother.

"Zack, when are you going to make me happy?"

"Uh?" Zack halted in surprise.

"You know." His mother pointed toward the ceiling. "Naomi." She mouthed. Her eyes lit up with a heady grin. "Come on, don't play shy with me."

"Gosh, Mom, you can't rush things."

"Look, at my age, you stop trying to take things slowly."

"You're beautiful regardless of your age."

"Keep the compliments coming. Your father could stand to learn a thing or two from his son. By the way, glad to see you two talking. He's so proud of you." She hugged him. "I've got to run, there's a sale at my favorite boutique."

He kissed her cheek. "See you later."

"Next time, it's my turn to have a chat with you. I want you all to myself. You can fill me in and tell me how much you love Naomi." She patted his cheek before walking away.

Chapter 11

The photographer and his small crew followed in a van. Naomi sat back in the SUV while Zack drove away from the city into the mountains. They passed large evergreen trees rooted into the ground like sentries guarding the land. An early-morning misty rain enveloped the vivid green landscape, making the area seem touched by faeries.

Later they passed vacation homes that peeked through the trees. The large windows caught the glint of the afternoon sun. Despite the dipping temperatures, the bright sunlight made it look like a summer day. She might not know a thing about photography, but she did know that a sunny day with few clouds couldn't be a bad thing.

"Here we are." Zack turned into a driveway and drove straight to the attached three car garage.

"Wow." Naomi's admiration waffled between the property or specifically the house.

Zack stuck his head out the window. "You can park here."

The photographer and his crew parked next to their vehicle. Their muted music blared when they opened the side door. Four men and a woman, the makeup artist, emerged.

"Let's head into the house." Zack led the way.

Naomi stayed behind for a few seconds to enjoy the large wraparound porch. She investigated all around, noting that each side of the house had a door that led onto the porch. The rocking chairs and swing chair added coziness to the setting. She imagined Zack and Chantelle coming here for family vacations. The house seemed like the perfect place for a family to enjoy.

"Hey, are you going to join us? Or are you waiting to meet some of our furry friends?"

Naomi screamed and ran toward the door. She punched Zack in the arm when he laughed at her.

"Lorenzo, you and your crew will be staying at the guesthouse in the back."

Naomi headed to the back of the house and almost gasped. The guesthouse was a duplex that could sit on any city block for young professionals. "I'm falling for this place hard."

"Thank my dad. He's a whiz at real estate and getting fantastic deals."

Naomi turned from the window. "You are too."

"Not lately."

Naomi didn't continue the conversation with the crew present. But she need not have worried, because the crew were equally wowed by the guest quarters and had gone through the back door.

"So where are you staying?" Naomi slid her hand against the high-end marble counter in the kitchen area.

"Don't even play with me. I've had this planned to snatch you away and have you for myself."

"Ooh, my alpha man, are you going to throw me over your shoulder and take me to your cave?"

"When the sun sets, you just wait."

Naomi giggled. She had missed his body covering hers and his attention to her every need. By her watch, she had a couple of hours before dusk.

The crew noisily entered through the back door. The five people talked at the same time, exclaiming about the place and their new home for the next several days.

"Can we get started now? I want to do some test shots," Lorenzo asked. "I won't take all night."

"Do I have do makeup, hair and all that?"

"No. Since we still have light, I want to go explore for good locations. If you're with me, I can also take a few shots to see if it works."

"Okay." Naomi didn't mind getting to work right away. She looked over to Zack to see if he minded.

"You go, earn a living. The other guys and I will make dinner."

"I'll go with them," Martha, the makeup artist, said.

"Cool. Let's go." Lorenzo jangled his keys.

"By the way, if you want to ride horses, there's a stable a mile down the road."

"Don't even think about it. My last horse ride was on a merry-go-round." Naomi shook her head.

"You don't have to ride, just pose."

"On a horse? You want me to break my neck. Zack, call my superagent."

"No, because I don't want Brent camping out."

"Okay, how about posing in front of the horse," Lorenzo asked.

"How about finding a log in the woods and I just stand and pose?"

Lorenzo shook his head. Armed with his camera, he headed out of the house. Naomi and Martha trailed as they chatted about the healthy condition of her skin.

"We'll head down to the end of this road, as Zack suggested." Lorenzo drummed his fingers along the steering wheel. "Are you excited about this?"

"Kind of. How about you?"

"I'm stoked. You'll be awesome. When I looked at the photos from the fundraiser party, I had that feeling that I normally get when I discover a rare beauty."

"Pressure!" Naomi wished she could pull down the visor and look into the mirror. She wanted to see what he saw.

"I'm looking forward to trying a few new eye designs."

"Nothing too weird. I'm not doing avant-garde."

"I'd like to be recognizable." Naomi tended to wear makeup when she had a formal function to attend. Otherwise, she used soap and water and a light lip gloss as her usual daily wear.

"I'm going to park here. I see a spot already." Lorenzo hopped out the van and headed into the woods.

"Is he always this hyper? It's like being locked in a room of a hyper teen."

"He's harmless," Martha explained. "He loves photographing models. Got him in trouble when he was in high school. People thought he was just trying to be fresh."

"You know a lot about him."

"He's my younger brother. I do the makeup and he takes the photos."

Naomi looked at Martha for the first time, noting the similarities. She'd never have guessed they were siblings. She found their relationship comforting.

"Let's go find him before he loses us or his way." Naomi followed the path that she saw Lorenzo head down.

The foliage wasn't friendly, with large, protruding tree trunks and thick, mossy underbrush that was slippery.

"Lorenzo?"

"Over here."

Naomi turned toward the sound of his voice. She and Martha climbed over huge boulders and stood looking down at a serene paradise. A small river snaked through the land adding its own decorative power. Too bad the sounds of the environment weren't going to be recorded. The thrilling tweets of the birds, along with the lazy winding fall of the water against the rocks and general calls of the wild would fit an audio track for outdoor listening pleasure.

Lorenzo snapped several photos with and without her. Martha stepped in to provide her input. Together they managed to get samples of satisfactory shots. More important, she enjoyed every painstaking minute of the process.

"Tomorrow, you may not be smiling at the end," Martha warned as they made their way back to the house.

"She's not kidding. I'll be very exact. My crew will probably want to toss me off a cliff. You may want to quit."

"I'm a big girl. I don't tend to buckle under pressure."

"Cool. That's what I like to hear."

They blasted the radio and sang at the top of their voices. Naomi couldn't believe how her life had changed in a short space of time. Playing Superwoman certainly had its rewards.

Zack waited on the porch rocking in one of the many chairs. Dinner was done. The crew had eaten and headed back to their quarters. Now he waited for Naomi. He would finally have her to himself. They could have a candlelit dinner before he scooped her into his arms.

He heard the van before it turned into the driveway. The music blared, but the sounds of their voices contributing to the din made him smile. Judging from their smiles, he suspected that they had a successful first day of test shooting.

"I'm starved," Naomi exclaimed. She ran up to him and kissed him squarely on the mouth.

Heaven help him. Thank goodness for her sake there were witnesses to any acts of seduction.

"Something smells fantastic."

"Help yourself. Your other crew members took their food and left."

"Why are you chasing them away?" Naomi whispered.

"Only two options exist."

"A slow seduction without curious eyes. Or a public spectacle."

"I would test you, but I don't trust you not to try and make a point. So I'm going for choice A."

Obviously, Lorenzo and Martha got the hint. They packed their plates with hot dogs, roasted corn on the cob and baked beans. With a cheery goodbye, they left.

"I'll lock up." He headed for the front door.

"I'll clean up. Doesn't look like much, since they used paper products."

Zack locked the doors and windows and then turned on the security alarm.

"Are you sure you're only trying to keep out the burglars?" She sashayed up to him. "Maybe you're trying to keep me in."

"There are other ways to have you stay put." He walked up behind her at the sink and twisted the blind closed.

She arched her back against him, swinging her hips from side to side against his pelvis. He trailed a finger up her spine, enjoying the twitches of her body.

His hands worked the muscles near her shoulder radiating outward to her arms. He loved touching her skin. Gently he laid his forehead against the back of her head, inhaling her smooth scent.

She turned suddenly. Zack placed two small kisses on her chest.

"Let's head upstairs." She moaned as his lips brushed her nipple.

He lifted her against his chest. She wrapped her arms around his neck. With little effort, he mounted the stairs and headed upstairs to the master suite. He knew she hadn't seen the rooms.

Tonight only one room mattered.

He placed her gently onto the bed but didn't release her until he kissed her squarely on the mouth.

"Do you want to see some of the lingerie?"

"I won't refuse, although I hold no promises that you'll be wearing it for any length of time."

"Go away." She waved him away. "I want it to be a surprise."

Zack took the wait time to clean up.

"Ready."

He entered the room, now bathed in muted light. Naomi sat against the pillows in a soft beige silk lingerie with delicate lacing. Her skin glowed, the muscular, toned legs drawn up where she sat. She'd fluffed her hair into a wild mane framing her slender face. Lip gloss turned her mouth into a sexy pout.

Zack took his time walking to the bed. He could have launched himself like a kid playing Superman to land on the bed next to Naomi. Instead he slowly unbuttoned his shirt and tossed it aside.

She crawled on her knees toward him. That wicked smile made him want to melt.

"I want to do that." She brushed his hand aside from his pants. She kissed his stomach, smiling wickedly when the muscles crunched as his breath hitched. He balled his hands into fists to keep from grabbing her head.

Her hands unfastened his pants and then unzipped the opening. Complete with a giggle, she bit her bottom lip while her hand slipped into his pants and cupped him.

He was already aroused. Her personal attention solidified his commitment to the moment. When she eased her hand into his underwear, he jerked back.

"Shh." She attempted to soothe him but was having the opposite effect.

His hands could no longer stay at his sides. He grabbed her arms to hold her still. He couldn't take one more stroke against his arousal. He couldn't survive her tongue addressing his stomach.

"So you like what you see?" Naomi looked up at him.

Zack released her arms. He took a step back, not too

much because he didn't want the air to cool the warmth that they generated between them.

"You'll be posing in this?"

"Yep. Something along these lines." She raised up on her knees. Her fingers slid the edges of the lingerie up her legs. The movement was slow, deliberate, teasing.

Her quadriceps flexed and relaxed as she moved.

The hemline continued its ascent until the apex between her legs made a bold presentation. He reached for her, but she scooted back, providing him with a broader view of the final treasure.

She smiled, teasing him with her tongue brushing over her top lip. He rested his knee on the edge of the bed, trying to keep up with her game.

On her back, she pulled up the hem to her hip.

"Think you're up to satisfying me?"

"You're kidding, right?" She had no idea what a dangerous game she played with him.

Naomi straddled her legs open, drawing up one on top of the other. "I'm pretty hungry tonight. I'm just trying to make sure that you can take care of fulfilling any seconds."

Zack saw the flickers of desire radiate in Naomi's face. Her body looked ripe for the plucking, and he was straining against his willpower as he watched her stroke the tender flesh between her legs.

He grabbed her ankles and pulled her toward him. At the last minute, he flipped her over, enjoying the sight of her round buttocks facing him. He stroked the length of her legs, massaging her behind as she whimpered. Now it was his turn to stroke and cajole her body to respond for him.

He kissed her bud, flicking her essence with his

tongue. She cried out softly in the pillow. He stroked her gently, creating his own rhythm to stir her passion.

Her moist state excited him further. But he wasn't done taking her near the peak. His fingers took charge, slipping in to play with that mysterious spot that heightened her pleasure to epic levels.

Her cries grew more intense and she rocked back and forth under his ministrations. He felt her tighten against his touch.

Gently he turned her over and slid the lingerie completely off. Her breasts, pert and aroused, cushioned his face. While he took her nipple into his mouth, he entered between her legs with a powerful thrust. She moaned and hooked her legs around his hips.

Zack grabbed the sheets and continued thrusting in perfect match with Naomi's grinding movements. He buried his head against her long neck. Her entire body had the power to arouse him.

Her hands slid along his back. Her legs tightened around his hips. He sensed the proximity of her climax. Together they jumped headlong, tumbling and rolling through the waves of desire. Each wave roared in, growing stronger and more fierce.

"I love you, Zack," Naomi softly said.

His eyes shot open. The release burst from him meeting hers halfway. The intensity brought difficulty, seeing, hearing and even breathing. His heart pounded in his head.

Had he imagined it all?

Chapter 12

Zack looked over the top of the newspaper to spy. Naomi ate a small breakfast as she read through paperwork. All appeared normal. She'd kissed him when she came down to eat. Patted his behind with a devilish grin and grabbed a strip of bacon to munch on until everything was done cooking.

Did his mind want to hear her utter those three words? Was it all one-sided on his part to play the role of a lovesick puppy?

"Are you all set?" he asked, still trying to read her body language.

"Yep. You are going to come this time."

"Sure. I don't want to miss it."

"Plus I want your input."

"I don't think the photographer wants me butting into his world. I wouldn't appreciate it if the roles were reversed."

"You've got a point." She set down her pen. "But since when did I play by the rules?" She stretched and yawned. "Chop-chop, get dressed."

Zack looked down at the T-shirt and pajama bottoms. The woman had him in a daze. Now he'd have to hurry.

"Here come the rest of the crew."

"You go with them. I'll catch up to you."

"No, I'll wait."

"Remember what I said about butting into other people's business. This is Lorenzo's deal."

"Okay." She opened the back door for the crew, who piled into the kitchen. Naomi exclaimed when the breeze blew in, "It's freezing out there."

"Temperature's plummeted." Lorenzo didn't mince words.

"And you want me to go sit on a rock and look like I'm one with nature?"

"Yep."

Zack tried to hide his chuckle but failed miserably. "I'll go get dressed and catch up with you."

"You'd better." Naomi made a face at him.

Zack headed upstairs for a quick shower. He did want to be on the shoot with Naomi. She'd shared her world with him with no hesitation. Knowing how hard she had to push to get him to open up, he felt guilty at the double standard.

After a quick, hot shower, he dressed in a turtleneck and jeans and his boots. He'd felt the blast of cold air when he was sitting at the table. Considering how long they would be outdoors, he'd better insulate.

He'd have to fight the urge to scold the photographer for keeping Naomi in the cold. She wasn't the first model to deal with the elements for the perfect shot. But unlike other models, she was his woman. He felt the need to protect.

Shortly the sound of the car pulling out of the driveway announced their departure. The house was eerily quiet. He did like having the boisterous company. Friends did matter. Family was important.

He was ready to leave. Now he couldn't find the car keys. All the usual places didn't reveal anything. Maybe Naomi took them by mistake. He kept hunting, ending at the table.

Naomi's papers were still there spread out like a fan. He glanced at them as he patted around them for his keys. The papers were a copy of the insurance forms from a woman who made Naomi the beneficiary. The million-dollar policy had a paper clip attached to the top of the page. Next to the paperwork, a handwritten note was set aside.

He didn't read the note but couldn't help wondering who the woman was. Naomi's past was fuzzy. As he tried to recall what he knew, the only person who stood out prominently was her grandmother. He'd only heard about her ailing grandfather. But really no one else had gotten a mention by her.

Maybe she didn't want to share that part of her. How could he complain?

He continued looking for his keys. He put on his coat to search on the porch. The minute he swung the coat over his shoulders, he heard the telltale jingle. He looped the key ring around his finger and then locked the house.

"About time," Naomi mumbled when Zack stepped out of the SUV. She shivered beneath the heavy down coat. The covering didn't help. Cold was cold. The little space heater in the van no longer warmed her cold fingers and toes. Many of the shots were unusable because she clenched her jaw to keep from chattering.

"How's it going?"

"I think we're going to have to take to the indoors and hope that the temperature goes up a bit tomorrow."

"And if it doesn't?" Naomi knew they had only planned to stay for two days.

Lorenzo didn't respond. The tip of his nose took on a pink hue. His cheeks were red. Even he shivered and he was covered from head to toe.

Martha stepped into her view. "I need to touch up your makeup."

Naomi shrugged. She hadn't done anything to wear off the thick layer of base.

"You've got to think about something that warms you. Pick a place that represents paradise. The sun is beaming. The sand is hot under your feet. You want the sun to bathe your limbs. And you're preening under the warmth. You want all your admirers to look at your long, graceful physique. You want them to desire you and soak you up like a tall glass of water for a thirsty man. You're beautiful. You're gorgeous. You're sexy as hell." She dabbed the lipstick brush in the palette and painted her lips. She looked over her shoulder. "Sensual, tasteful, provocative. Make Zack hot for you." Martha snapped the compact shut. "Okay, Lorenzo, she's ready."

"Damn, you're good." Naomi had begun to believe everything Martha said. Her cheeks even warmed at the thought of arousing Zack. Sure enough, the thought had banished the reality of the cool climate.

Lorenzo nodded to his sister and moved the camera into place. He shouted a few directions to his crew. They moved around for the next round of shots.

Naomi opened the coat and stepped out. She was ready. She kept Martha's words in the forefront of her thoughts. As she moved into position, she found Zack standing behind Lorenzo. He was true to his word that he wouldn't intrude on the other man's space.

She didn't need him to intrude. Instead, she focused on his face, but not today when he looked pensive and preoccupied. She wanted the face of the man who touched her with the knowledge of how to please her. She sought the face of the man who could be romantic and tentative to assertive and intoxicating to her system. The man who made her last reserve crumble to admit her love in a strangled whisper.

Naomi followed Lorenzo's directions to curve her back, lower her jaw, relax her elbow, elongate her fingers, now arch her back, straighten her leg, no, the other leg.

"Relax!" Lorenzo shouted. His camera hung from around his neck as though it had also quit with her latest performance.

Naomi's eyebrow shot up. She was trying her best. What did he want? She already felt like a rag doll.

"Are you going to work me over again?" she said to Martha, who fussed with her hair.

"You were doing fine and then suddenly you tensed up. Go back to the happy thoughts. Whatever you segued to isn't going to win you any points with Lorenzo."

"I'm about to have a fit with your brother."

"I would say go for it, but from experience, I'd have to say that you'd lose the fight. He's known to throw a B-fit, if you know what I mean."

"Well, from one B to another, let him bring it on." Naomi marched toward the van. She needed to sit in front of the heater. Lorenzo would have to wait.

Lorenzo apparently wasn't having it. He shouted more instructions to his crew. They madly scrambled toward the van with her.

Lorenzo kept snapping. Nodding, pleased with whatever was happening. Naomi didn't care, she sat in the driver's seat and turned on the heat to full blast. She leaned back and closed her eyes imagining her entire body thawing.

The whir of the camera sounded in her ear. She slowly opened eyes to see Lorenzo inches away from her cheek, the camera closing in even more.

"Open your mouth slightly. Lick your lips so they're moist."

She complied. The man was relentless.

"Stare straight ahead."

Zack stood in front of the SUV grinning. His shoulders shook with his full-out laugh.

Naomi fastened on that mouth and imagined biting on his lip before diving her tongue into his mouth. She wanted to erase that grin and make him groan under her control.

"Yes, that's the look I want."

Naomi blocked out Lorenzo.

Zack in his black turtleneck with black jeans and black boots with his coat opened looked unforgettably sexy. She wanted to jump his bones right there in the van minus the crew. She broadcast her thoughts with all the telepathic powers she could muster.

His smile grew smaller. His eyes narrowed. She saw him shift his stance. His nerves must have unsettled him. He nibbled at his lip and finally folded his arms across his chest, as if in effort to remain still.

Naomi let a small smile curl and linger on her lips.

"Okay, turn slightly."

She responded, not wanting to tear her gaze from Zack.

"Cool. We got our shot." Lorenzo straightened up. His characteristic lopsided grin was back in place. "Tomorrow we'll go for some indoor shots. You were fantastic today."

All the bustle around her as the equipment was packed and loaded into the van nipped at the bubble she'd created between Zack and her. She saw him talking with Lorenzo, looking completely unaffected by all her hot thoughts. Well, at least it had been nice for her.

Naomi slipped on her clothes in the back of the van. Then she emerged to look for Zack. Now he was talking to some of the crew. She headed over to stand at his side.

"Hey, gorgeous."

"Like you noticed," she remarked, surprised by her own irritation that her sexy come-hither looks had no effect on him.

"I noticed too much." He grabbed her and planted a kiss.

Naomi slipped her arms under his coat. She laid her cheek against his chest and pressed her ear to listen to his heartbeat. The rumble of his voice made it difficult. Yet she wanted to stay in that position, preferably horizontally.

"Want to go to dinner?"

She nodded, only releasing him then. "What about the others?"

"I only promised them a roof over their heads. The meals have been a treat. They can fend for themselves for one day."

"See you tomorrow," Lorenzo called out as he headed to his van.

"I think you got yourself a number-one fan."

"You're exaggerating. I think he wanted to strangle me and I wanted to kill him."

"It did get heated. I'd never seen you so fierce." He had his arm around her as they went to his SUV. He growled at her before he got in the car.

"You've never seen my games."

"Remind me never to make you angry."

She stroked his head, loving the small tight curls of his hair. He was always groomed with a slight bad-boy edge to his fashion. "I think you would look good in front of the camera."

"Oh, no, don't even think about it." Zack took his eyes off the road.

"We can do a fashion layout together like that soccer guy and his ultra-skinny wife."

"How many ways to say no?" Zack pressed on the accelerator. "Time to get some food in front of you. Need to keep you from strategizing my future."

"Consider it like pocket money. Real-estate developer, model and—" Naomi stopped herself from saying "ultimate boyfriend." She'd entered this thing between them, whatever it was, with no illusions. Just because she wanted to change the rules didn't mean that she had to follow her heart. She'd rather enjoy what she had now than risk rejection. Her heart would just have to deal.

"Don't go quiet on me. I love hearing your crazy thoughts and fantasies."

"The crazy thought right now is how hungry I am. I want comfort food. Nothing fancy. Nothing I can't pronounce. I want some good old-fashioned carbs and a decadent dessert."

"Your wish is mine to fulfill." He nodded at her with his hand over his heart.

She wanted to put her hand over his heart and lay claim to it.

Zack sat back stuffed from the hearty vegetable soup and ham-and-cheese sandwich. The deli meat had been piled over an inch thick with the freshly baked bread. He grinned as Naomi shook her head at the waiter's offer to bring the dessert menu.

"I feel like a slug." She propped her chin in her hand.

"You've had quite a day. You need a good long soak and a massage," Zack advised.

"Don't tease me."

"I'm not. My hands are magical." He rubbed his hands together.

"Let's not talk about hands."

"I know you'd rather I did a show-don't-tell." He loved the way she closed her eyes with a soft smile as he talked. "You know I could make you confess."

"Go ahead. I have nothing to confess."

He wanted to ask her about the woman listed on the paperwork, but he couldn't intrude on her life or demand anything. He'd done his fair share to keep parts of his life separate and private.

She opened her eyes. "You're easy. I would've continued to pry to get some juicy stuff. We've all got something tucked away."

"That's probably a good thing." He thought of his own circumstances.

Naomi drew up. Her brow crinkled as she thought. "We can't say we're sharing in each other lives if we constantly hide parts of ourselves from each other."

"Sometimes the time isn't right."

Naomi shrugged. Her eyes examined him. He could practically hear her analyze his comments.

"Let's go." He broke the spell.

"Sure."

They headed back to the house subdued and thoughtful. Zack wished he hadn't pushed for an opening to inquire about Naomi's business. Now he came across as someone who'd rather keep secrets. His life wasn't about hiding, but rather avoiding people's conclusions, which had a way of ending with rejection or judgment.

As soon as they were back in the house, Naomi hung up her coat, then excused herself for the soak. Zack noted that she didn't invite him to join her or send any sexy coded looks. Although he wasn't sure what caused the cool attitude, he knew that he'd contributed to it.

His cell phone rang. Brent's name lit up the display screen. Bad timing. He wanted to go up to Naomi and talk.

"Hey, man, what's up?"

"Got some information for you."

"About Lassiter?"

"No. The other thing. Your birth mother in Haiti."

Zack walked to the couch, his knees felt as if they'd give out. His stomach clenched, along with his hand holding the phone.

"You there, buddy?"

"Yeah," his voice croaked.

"I found the information, not only her name, but where she lives."

Zack closed his eyes. He could have pursued this information at any time but hadn't. Having Naomi in his life eased aside the hesitation. Could it be that after all these years, he'd get to meet his birth mother? Was he happy? Was he sad? Did he want to dredge up anger for being given away? Or should he allow the guilt for wanting to know his birth mother slow the revelation to the only people whom he knew as his family?

"Hey, Zack, you want me to call you back later?"

"No. Sorry. The news caught me off guard." He looked around for a pen, taking the one from Naomi's spot at the table. He wrote the information, folded the paper and kept it in his hand.

"Call me when you get back into town. I'm here if you need anything, man."

Zack thanked him and ended the call.

The floorboard overhead creaked. Naomi must be out of the shower. He paused at the bottom of the step. He wanted to immediately make plans to head to Haiti. But he didn't want to disappoint her by not showing up to her shoot. He took the folded paper in his hand and shoved it into his pants pocket.

Pinning on a bright smile, he ran up the stairs. "I hope you're indecent tonight."

"Not before I receive my massage, Mr. Man."

Chapter 13

Naomi made it through the photo shoot with fewer lectures from Martha and with some favorable nods from Lorenzo. She felt good with herself for being able to respond to the directions with her own style. Although the temperature didn't feel any different from the previous day's frigid weather, she liked her new outfit of a flannel pajama bottom, bunny slippers and a tank top that left little to the imagination.

Where Zack had remained in center focus yesterday, today he leaned against his car looking off into the distance. Her challenge was not to allow any insecurity to creep in. Their lovemaking last night had been tender, sweet. Not that she had any complaints. But this morning when she thought she could roll over and entice him for an encore, he was already gone from the bed.

Yet she couldn't point to one specific thing that made her feel off-kilter. Their breakfast was quiet. He answered her questions, laughed when appropriate, nodded as she talked about general topics.

Naomi shifted poses, self-correcting her arms. She maintained focus on the camera lens as Lorenzo moved in for several close-up shots. Happy thoughts. Contentment. Love.

"You're looking fantastic today. You look vulnerable, sweet. Huggable."

Naomi blinked away the tears that had shown up on the last shot. She was determined not to have a meltdown. Even if she did turn into an emotional puddle, Zack wouldn't notice. He was clearly more interested in the paper that he repeatedly read before folding it and putting it in his pocket. Her confidence didn't improve when he looked at his watch, then leaned over to Martha.

Naomi approached him. "I can get a ride back with the guys if you have to be somewhere else."

"No. I can wait."

"What's the matter?" Naomi touched his arm.

"Business. Something came up."

She waited to see if he would share with her. His mouth tightened as if to ensure that he didn't say anything.

"Lorenzo is waiting for you. You're doing great." He leaned to kiss her mouth, but she turned her head a smidgen. He caught the corner of her mouth.

Naomi wanted to get into it right there. But professionalism dictated otherwise. She blew out her cheeks to ward off any tightness in her face. What the heck was happening? Right before her eyes, he seemed to be retreating. Did this quick trip make things too hot and heavy between them? Was he putting space where she wanted to close and secure against any gaps?

* * *

Finally the photo shoot ended. Champagne was popped for the nondrivers. Naomi sipped in celebration for taking the risk to do something new. Zack remained in the background, still reserved but occasionally offering a weak smile.

On the way back to his parents, Naomi couldn't take the strained silence anymore. If she'd done something to offend, then she was ready to make amends.

"What has you so quiet and pensive?" she asked.

"Not—"

"Look, before you raise your hand to proclaim your innocence, I know something is wrong. We are a work in progress, but I feel as though I know you well enough to sense when something is off." She rubbed his arm. "I don't mean to snap, but I'm here. My shoulders are strong and wide. I can handle just about everything. I've healed from a vicious assault."

He took her hand and kissed it. "You're right. I had Brent investigate the whereabouts of my mother."

"Frannie?"

"My birth mother."

"And you got information?"

Zack nodded.

"Why aren't you happy?"

"I'm not sure how I feel. Part of me is numb because I've wanted to know for such a long time. Part of me wants to scream, rage, laugh. I just don't know."

"You don't have to do anything right away."

"But I do. I want to go to Haiti as soon as possible."

"Oh." Naomi heard the eagerness to go on his quest. Alone.

"I've got to pack. Rachel will have to reschedule my

appointments for the rest of the week. Thank goodness I don't have any pets."

"What about your parents? You can't head off without talking to them." Her heart cried out on her behalf. But she would never put herself in the position to beg.

"I'll take care of it."

"You're sounding so cavalier." Naomi chanced a glance at him.

"Don't try to psychoanalyze. I'll let them know."

Naomi turned her attention to the fleeting landscape. Already the walls were being erected. Zack was returning to his comfort zone, closing the gate, pushing her out. She watched helplessly at the speed of its creation.

Silence reigned until Zack pulled up in front of the house. Before he could get out of the car, Naomi slid out. She walked quickly toward the house.

"Wait, Naomi."

She didn't stop right away. What more could he say? How else could he harm her? She tucked her hurt away and faced him.

"I have to talk to my parents tonight." He joined her where she stood. "I want to get a flight out within the next few days."

She turned and walked to the door. "How long will you be gone?"

"Don't know. If the information Brent gave me is correct, then it shouldn't take long." He opened the front door for her. "But I'm open for anything."

"Don't you want to feel out your parents before you share this? Did they know you were looking for information?"

"No. I don't know. But they should be happy for me."

"And I'm sure they will understand your need to

know. But there may be some other feelings that could rise to the surface feeding into doubts and possible insecurities." She continued, "You're asking a lot of the people who care about you."

"What about me?" He shoved his hands into his pocket. "Don't I have the right to want to find out about my past?"

"Sometimes I want to know about my mother. I kill the urge, partly out of obligation to my grandparents because they sacrificed to raise me. Another part of me doesn't want to know because then a door will open that I may not be able to close." She sighed, heavily. "My mother sent me a letter with a life insurance policy as if that will heal not having her in my life."

"Will you answer her?"

"I did. I told her that my grandmother deserved to be the beneficiary. I'm self-sufficient."

Zack pulled her in with his gaze. "Doesn't she have a right to know about you?"

The question hung in the air. Unanswered.

Naomi didn't want to argue. While she tried to get him to understand his parents' point of view, who was there to get him to understand hers?

"You're back." His father came forward and hugged him, then Naomi. "I want to hear the details." He hooked his hand through Naomi's arm. "Come join us in the family room." He called to his wife.

"Dad, let's all catch up a bit later. I've got something important to tell you." Zack reached out to her. But Naomi stepped back. She didn't agree with the delivery, knowing the pain of surprise would be sharper than what he actually was doing. She didn't want to be a tool of convenience. Clearly, he took her presence at the house to be a constant.

"I'll head up. I've got some paperwork to complete."

Zack stared at her but didn't stop her. She headed up the stairs, trying to organize her thoughts to determine her next step.

"Your mother's waiting." His father waited for him to refocus and follow him to the family room.

"Zack, good to see you. Where's Naomi?" His mother looked behind him.

"She's upstairs. But I want to talk to you."

"You look serious. Is it good news?" His mother wiggled her eyebrows. Hope clearly shone in her eyes.

Zack shook his head. He didn't want to be distracted from what he had to say. "It's about my birth mother."

His father's sharp inhalation made him hesitate. He remembered his father's strong caution—a caution he hadn't followed. He continued.

"I got information on my birth mother and possibly where she's located." He took his mother's limp hand. "I want to go find her."

His mother sat silently for an unbearable amount of time.

"I knew this day would come." His mom dabbed at the corners of her eyes. "I don't want you to think that I wouldn't have given you any information I had."

"I know," Zack said softly.

"Do you plan to go barge into her life?" His father's anger pulsed in the vein in his throat.

Zack hadn't thought that he'd be intruding. After all, he was the one left behind at the mission.

"Paul, calm down. Son," his mother's plea and use of the word stirred his regret, "I'm not going to stop you or even slow you. All I'm saying is that you be sure to have a Plan A if everything goes the way you have it planned in your mind. And have a Plan B if things take a detour."

Zack nodded. He hugged his mother, hoping his love could pour into her to set her mind at ease.

"Frannie can pretend that she's okay with this. I don't think you've taken everything into consideration."

"What is the problem, Dad?" Zack grew tired of his father's dire predictions.

"Paul, don't you dare make him feel like he wronged someone," Frannie warned.

"I hope you can come to understand why I need to do this." Zack kissed his mother's cheek and left the room. He paused in the foyer, debating if he should try to talk to Naomi. His hand brushed his pocket with the information.

He had to find his mother.

Naomi awoke the next morning after a restless night. She felt as if someone had bodyslammed her into the ground. Her eyes could barely open. She didn't have to look in the mirror to know that she looked a sight.

Now in the brightness of the morning, she was even more committed to her action. The fairy tale had to end. Although she had created a more upbeat ending, reality had thrust in an ugly alternative.

After she dressed, she headed down. The minute she descended the stairs, she sensed a difference in the air. A somber note hung over the area. No one was in sight or could be heard.

Naomi appreciated the quiet and helped herself to a bowl of oatmeal with a side of assorted fruits. She had to make a few calls as soon as she was done eating to start her new plan of action.

The back door opened and the Keathleys entered.

"Hi, sweetheart, how are you doing?"

"Hi, Frannie, I'm finishing up with breakfast."

"Good, glad you didn't skip it."

Naomi nodded, trying to smile along with Zack's mother.

"I'm heading upstairs." Paul didn't stick around to chit-chat.

"Frannie, you know that I appreciate all that you've done for me."

"Yes?" Frannie's frown lowered over her piercing gaze. "Don't tell me you're leaving."

"It's time for me to go home," she admitted, not able to hide the sadness from her voice.

"Did you have a fight with Zack?"

"No. He had nothing to do with my decision. Nothing can take away or replace the wonderful opportunity to get to know your family. I will treasure it always, but it's time to return home."

"Sit down."

Naomi shook her head. She couldn't possibly sit in front of this kind woman and talk about her feelings. She didn't have the stamina to put on a brave face when all she wanted to do was dissolve into tears.

"I know my son hurt you."

"He doesn't know," Naomi said softly.

"Which makes it that much worse."

"I never want to be the type of woman who holds her man back because she's afraid of the future. We had fun together."

"He loves you, Naomi."

"Sometimes, that's not enough." She didn't have the heart to argue with his mother that her son didn't love her.

"Will you wait for him to return from Haiti?"

"I can't." She had no desire to look like a forlorn house pet waiting for attention.

"When will you leave?"

"In a few days."

"My son is a fool."

"He believes in what he's doing."

"Please stay in touch."

"Sure thing, Frannie."

Naomi headed back upstairs and started making her calls. She called her sorors to update them and alert them that she'd be home soon. Then she called Brent to explain that she was returning home. Everyone sounded disappointed, but the more people she told, the easier her story became.

Now the final thing to do was to call the airline. She waited on hold listening to the various choices and the buttons she had to push.

Fifteen minutes later, she had a window seat in the front part of the plane. Now she could say that she was definitely returning home.

Her heart ached for having to take that step. As she pulled out her suitcase to begin packing, the tears fell hot and poignant. Love wasn't supposed to hurt. She'd worked hard to make sure that she remained levelheaded and not sappy over any man. However, Zack wasn't any man.

As she packed souvenirs that she'd bought, each knickknack brought back tender memories of time shared with Zack. She'd cut her losses and hold on to the happy times.

Zack drank a strong cup of black coffee, no milk, no sugar. He didn't bother to sleep, knowing that his mind wouldn't shut off. He sat in the deli watching other patrons come and go.

"Lost your way?"

Zack looked over his shoulder and immediately broke into a grin. "Hey, Brent, following me?"

"I stopped by your house this morning. Figured since you didn't return my call, I'd have to track you. You were supposed to contact me when you got back from the photography shoot."

"All kinds of hell broke loose. Parents freaked."

"And Naomi?"

"She's fine."

"You don't think that she deserves an explanation?"

"I told her what was happening."

"Did you share how she could be a part of one of the most important moments of your life?"

"I didn't think that she'd be interested."

"I think that it was more about not releasing control. Once a control freak, always one."

"I see the conversation is deteriorating. I suppose my father has your ear and would rather that you talked me into staying and erasing the development from my memory."

"You sound paranoid. Get over yourself. I'm your friend and will always be your friend. It also means that I will not sit on the side and let you stomp over people."

"Thanks for the vote of confidence," Zack said wryly.

Brent sighed. "The reason that I stopped by was to offer my private plane."

"Thanks, man."

"I want you to chase the demons and hopefully don't have them turn on you."

"When have you gotten so philosophical? It's not like you're leading by example. Where's the woman in your life, since you're so full of advice, or just full of it?"

Brent moved his hands off the table as the waitress set down his mug of steaming coffee. He looked out the window, his jaw worked.

Zack wished he could withdraw the question and erase the manner in which he asked. There was no mistaking the pain that resonated off Brent's features.

"It'll be three years since Marjorie died. I wished you'd met her. She was crossing the road and a drunk driver with his third DUI murdered her. Took her life like that." He snapped his finger. "My life changed. How I think. How I feel. What I want. Every day is a struggle against the bitterness. I want his family, the drunk driver's, to feel one small part of the pain I feel."

"Brent, I wish I'd known."

"I shut myself off from everyone when I was successful. Didn't really reach out to my old friends until after everything went down. For that I'm sorry." He sipped his coffee, then said, "But this is why I know what I'm talking about. I pray for a miracle to turn back the clock, at least to give me the opportunity to say what's in my heart and not to hold back."

"I hope that one day you can move on. Having someone in your life is important. Kind of keeps you sane."

"And that's my message to you." Brent pointed at him.

Chapter 14

Zack hadn't gotten over Brent's heart-wrenching story. The timing of when Brent reentered his life was after his wife's death. He wished that he'd known so that he could have offered solace.

Now Brent's message stuck in his head with the replay button pressed down. He had a lot of thinking to do. What better place to go and think than in church? Plus Reba had told him that his mother was working here this afternoon.

He headed down the short hallway looking into the various offices. She assisted the office manager with a variety of duties. Then he heard her voice and laughter before he turned into the doorway.

"Zack, what are you doing here?" his mother teased. "You do know that it's not Sunday."

"Yes, Mom, you're very funny." He waited for her to invite him into the office.

"Stella, could you answer the phone? I need a few minutes with Zack."

She walked with him until she found an empty storage closet.

"Mom, about Haiti—"

"Listen, Zack, your father went into overprotective mode for my sake. I acted like a deer in the headlights, not knowing which way to go with your news. But this is your life. We shared our love and home with you as a family should do. How can I turn my back on you now? This is a time when you will need us the most."

Zack hugged his mom. "I'm going to look pretty strange crying on my mother's head in the supply closet."

"We'll make up a really good story for the gossipers."

He looked into the eyes of the woman who'd raised him. "I love you, Mom."

"I know, Son. I love you with all my heart." She touched his cheek. "You've got to tell Chantelle too. You all are close and she'd be hurt that you didn't tell her."

"Yeah, but she'll probably be madder that she can't go with me," he joked.

"Please do not let that child skip classes to go with you. If anyone should go it should be Naomi."

"You too?" He sighed and shook his head.

"Your father said the same thing?"

"No. Brent."

"Smart boy." Her thoughtful look crossed her face. "Another one who needs to settle down with a nice girl like—"

"I know, like Naomi. You've never gone crazy over anyone that I've brought home before."

"You're right. Some of those didn't deserve to be brought home. But Naomi touched me from the first time I saw her. She risked her life for my daughter. And her grandmother is good people." She held his face with a firm grip. "Seriously, Zack, don't let fear screw up your life."

Zack nodded. Easier said.

He left his mother, promising to call her every day when he left. Talking to her set aside a lot of the doubts over his actions. His mother had never been shy about talking to him on any subject. Her strength came through when he listened to her retell the stories of how she and his father struggled in the beginning of their marriage.

Money was tight and not always there. The pressure to have a family right away sometimes tore them apart. But remembering why they fell in love always brought them back together. He didn't have to go far from home for life lessons.

Without calling ahead, he drove across the city to the downtown business district. His father's company was in a high-rise building that also housed a major financial services company, a branch of a Fortune 100 computer firm and the regional office of a bank. His father's mega success had earned him a place among the rich and powerful in the Seattle area.

Zack parked in the spot that was once his. The parking space still carried his name with the open invitation from his father to rejoin the company. He turned off the engine.

Although he had suffered a few setbacks, Zack refused to quit and give up on himself. Knowing that the empty pieces of his life were about to be filled, he felt empowered. His determined footsteps echoed off the concrete walls in the underground parking lot.

"Good morning, Zack."

"Hi, Mrs. Vaughn, I'm here to see my dad."

"He's in a meeting, but it should be over shortly. You can wait here, if you don't mind."

Zack agreed. He made small talk with the office receptionist, catching up on her life with her third husband and blended family. No matter how much drama her life seemed to attract, she always had a sunny disposition that was infectious. Shortly thereafter, he was laughing at one of her stories.

The entry door leading to the interior of the office opened. His father's executive assistant appeared in the doorway. She held the door opened for a man who had his back to him but seemed familiar.

"Ah, Zack, you're here to see your father?"

"Yes, Mrs. Percy." Zack approached the door. His eyes remained on the man, who slowly turned. "Mr. Lassiter, what are you doing here?"

"Welcoming new opportunities." He smiled and walked past him. With a pinched, heavily lined face like his, Lassiter looked even more sinister when he smiled.

Zack wanted to follow him to the elevator and inquire further, but Mrs. Percy waited for him. He shook off his disquiet and allowed Mrs. Percy to escort him to see his father.

"I'm glad you stopped by. Your mother has worn my ear with a proper scolding or two."

"Dad, why was Lassiter here?" Zack opted to jump right in. "Plus, he looked quite pleased with himself."

"I had to offer something to get him to back off your deal."

"That's like getting in bed with the enemy."

"I can use Lassiter's influence on the low-income projects that I'm about to bid. Since we're at the same age group and similar background, I was able to appeal to his—charitable side," he said slyly.

"I wouldn't trust him."

"Don't worry. I'm a crafty one, too."

"Scary is more like it." Zack flopped down on the leather couch. He opened one of the bottled waters that his father always kept handy. "I stopped by for a specific reason."

"Go on." His father joined him with his own bottled water.

"I'm tidying the mess I made with my news. I'll be leaving for Haiti by tomorrow now that Brent will loan me his plane."

Paul paused. "I was hoping that you'd rethought your decision."

Zack didn't expect his father's position to remain adamantly opposed to his plans. Frankly, he expected the same reception that his mother gave him.

"I guess that I was wrong in thinking you'd come to your senses." His father continued to look at him.

The scene reminded him of the numerous times he'd had to have a father-and-son chat, usually after progress reports and final report cards were issued. That disapproving look that could make him feel small and guilty.

Zack shook off any sense of wrongdoing. "Dad, listen to me. I may have done a few stupid things in my life. I may have misread situations. I may not know everything, but I don't want to fight about this. I don't want the family split apart because I'm doing this. Why are you so against it?"

"I believe that adoptions are private arrangements. And like attorney-client, doctor-patient relationships, what was done, the reasons for it and all related matters, should stay behind closed doors," Paul said forcefully before speaking in a softer tone. "Nothing is ever as simple as we think. To believe that you can make such an announcement, then shoot off and plunk yourself down in someone's life with no thought as to the consequence for each step is self-indulgent."

Zack stared at his father, who rarely got so animated.

"I don't know how to convince you that I need to do this," Zack argued. "Privacy and confidential concerns are necessary, but I'm also part of the arrangement. I don't know if this woman will want to meet me. Maybe she has moved on with her life and I'm an unpleasant memory. But a part of me is very optimistic of the outcome. The first five years of my life is a part of who I am. I grew up thinking that it had to be swept under the rug and that I was supposed to turn my back on my past. I want to know her for all the right reasons."

His father rubbed his forehead, a sure sign that he was frustrated and highly irritable. "Well, I don't care what you find or think you need to know. I am your father. You are my son." He took a long drink from the water bottle.

Zack didn't know how to respond. There had never been a situation between his father and him that wasn't resolved. Either he capitulated or he was able to swing his father to his point of view. This new situation created a strange tension. "I want your approval."

"Like my blessing?"

Zack nodded.

"You'll go even if I don't give it."

Zack nodded.

His father sighed. "Okay. I'm here if you need me."

Zack believed what his father said. Now it made more sense. His father liked being in the position to catch him when he faltered. Through his life and with his company, his father always stepped up to right any wrongs, whether they were his fault or not. For once, his father couldn't help make things right.

"As soon as you return, you have to come over for a family dinner."

"Yes, sir." Zack leaned back in the couch. Now he could relax and enjoy his visit with his dad. "Are you free for lunch?"

"Let me check. I'll reschedule, if I have to. I have another subject to bring up."

"Yes?"

"Naomi."

Zack nodded. He couldn't get away from the mounds of advice.

The early afternoon slipped in with Zack feeling very satisfied. Lunch with his father had been like old times, with much laughter and his father's old-fashioned ideas on life and love. Though he teased his father, he shared his view that love required commitment.

One more stop and then he could call it a day. He headed to the city council office. His visit was unannounced, but he would rely on his name to get him into the council members' offices to meet with their staff.

His father had done the legwork of finding out about the origins of the audit. With his connection, he'd also managed to get the council to close the investigation without any conditions.

He felt nothing but gratitude for his father's actions, but he needed to show his face. He was his company. If he wanted to be successful in this town, he needed to do the meet and greet necessary to form alliances.

After the requisite information was collected by the receptionist, he waited for the legislative assistant of the chairman's office.

"Zack, come in. Good to see you."

"Mr. Peters, I'm glad to see you," he greeted the councilman. "I won't keep you."

"Actually, I'm glad you stopped in. I had the pleasure of talking with your father not too long ago."

"Yes, he told me." Zack tried to read if there were any hidden messages in the councilman's words.

"Unfortunately, I'm heading out to a meeting. Care to walk with me to my car?"

"Not a problem." Actually, the abbreviated visit worked for Zack, since he only wanted to shore up his connection with the council. The hard work of schmoozing would continue in earnest when he returned from Haiti.

"You know we have put the project up for rebid."

"Yes. Not happy about it."

"Too much controversy, otherwise. You can still submit a bid."

"I'll have to think about it. I'm sure there will be other projects on the horizon that will be of interest." Zack considered the possibility of collaborating with his father. Their combined knowledge and skills had strong potential. Excitement stirred within him.

They'd finally arrived at the car. Zack was parked on the next level up. He didn't need to see anyone else. Now he could go to Haiti without too much hanging over his head.

Even before the complete thought formed, he knew how untrue it was.

He had to talk to Naomi.

He reached for the cell phone and punched in the number. At the first ring, he ended the call. His mother's admonishment rang in his head. This situation didn't call for anything other than a face-to-face. Would she see him?

He dialed another number. He might need a bit of help.

"Reba, could I ask a favor?"

"Sure."

"Is Naomi there?"

"No. She stepped out earlier today and hasn't returned."

"Could you call me when she does return? It's important."

"Zack, I don't know if she'll return."

"What do you mean?"

"She had her suitcase with her. She told me that she wasn't leaving as yet."

"Does my mother know?" Zack couldn't imagine that Naomi would leave without telling his mother, and his mother had given no indication that she knew Naomi had left for good.

"No. She doesn't know."

"Well, don't alarm her. I'll come over for a little while in case Naomi comes in."

"Sure."

He hung up and drove a little faster to get to his parents' home. Although things had gotten tense between them, he'd never imagined that Naomi would leave without saying goodbye.

A touch of fear sent worrying thoughts that maybe

he'd pushed their relationship to a limit that she couldn't handle. There was so much he wanted to say. Now he prayed that he'd have the chance to say what was on his mind.

He arrived within the hour. Reba met him at the door. He didn't have to ask to know that Naomi hadn't returned. His call must have stirred her concern.

"Still haven't heard from her."

"May I go up to her room?"

"Sure. I hadn't thought to check on her items in there."

"Not your fault." He ran up the stairs, but then had to ask, "Which room?"

Reba directed him and he entered slowly. The room was neat and clean. He looked for any evidence that she'd left. He opened the closet and grew immediately perplexed. A small suitcase stood in the small area. Yet Reba mentioned seeing her leave with a suitcase.

He looked around a bit more carefully. The suitcase contained her clothing and toiletries. He noted that the case was already packed and not many personal items remained on the vanity.

"Any clues?" Reba stepped into the room and surveyed it.

"No."

Zack's glance swept the room and paused at the night-stand. He walked over, his forehead wrinkled at the sight of a small book on the otherwise empty area. The dark blue book looked like a journal. His hand paused over the cover as he sifted through various thoughts about whether to read it or not.

"The suitcase she used didn't have all these stickers. I would have remembered."

"Maybe she ran an errand and got caught up. Wouldn't be the first time."

Reba nodded, but didn't look convinced. "Come down and drink some tea with me."

"Please don't lecture me. It's been a long day. Everyone is on Team Naomi. I get it."

"Don't get defensive. I haven't had a chance to get you all to myself in a while."

"Sorry." He hadn't considered Reba's feelings at all. Zack didn't want to leave, but he couldn't really stay in Naomi's room.

"Are you here to set things right?"

"I hope so."

"There's the little boy I came to love. That expression should work," she nudged him.

Downstairs, he accepted the tea. Thankfully, Reba didn't push him for conversation. Did he dare leave without talking to her? Could he risk that she'd be here when he returned?

The front door opened. Zack and Reba hurried to the foyer. They both expressed their frustration when the new arrival happened to be Zack's mother. She stopped in surprise at their reaction.

"That's a first. I don't think that I've ever come home to find such an unwelcoming greeting."

"Sorry, Frannie," Reba answered. "We were waiting for Naomi."

"Oh, she called me to say that she was heading to the movies and dinner with a friend."

"A friend?" Zack didn't know of any friends in Seattle. Not that he was around Naomi all the time, but she'd never mentioned anyone. Now she was going to movies and dinner? That seemed a bit much for a casual acquaintance.

"I didn't ask for details. She's a grown woman." His mother paused. "Stop thinking the worst of people. I'm sure she's made friends with a few people here. I'm glad she's not cooped up like a princess locked in a castle waiting for you to come rescue her."

Zack didn't stick around much longer. He didn't know what time she'd return. He'd rather not sit around looking at his watch every other minute. Hopefully, tomorrow he'd get a chance to talk to her before having to head to Haiti.

Despite Reba and his mother's protests, he hugged them and then left. He'd had a long day full of closure and starting afresh. He was exhausted.

Chapter 15

Naomi pulled out her suitcase from the closet. She finished packing the remaining clothes, although she didn't have much. However, she'd accumulated a stockpile of computer games for when she had her away basketball games and a few items of clothing. Instead of dealing with the added weight, she'd taken the items to the post office.

A car horn sounded.

"Naomi, your ride is here."

Naomi headed for the stairs, taking her time down the steps with her suitcase.

"I'll see you in a bit, Reba."

"Have a safe trip."

"By the way, Zack called this morning to talk to you."

"What did you tell him?"

"That you'd left."

"Thanks." Naomi hoped that she was doing the right thing.

What wasn't going right was the weather. She wished that the day wasn't rainy. Flying in bad weather scared her. Having to make the trip in a small jet didn't help matters.

"I'll put your suitcase in the backseat. You're my kind of girl, who knows how to pack light." Brent met her at the door with an umbrella for shelter.

"You know I'm feeling mighty nervous."

"Understandable, but I guarantee that you'll be fine."

"You're like the man behind the curtain. Everyone's hopping to your beat, but they think it's their own thoughts."

"I'm not sure. Are you insulting me?"

Naomi laughed. "Just being honest."

"Okay." Brent laughed. "Now, let's get you to the airport."

Naomi tried to relax. She wanted to feel as confident as Brent seemed. As much as she tried, her stomach still stayed in knots. Plus she definitely couldn't copy the smile he wore.

"Zack called me a few minutes ago."

"He's making the rounds. He called Reba, too."

"Sounded like a lost puppy. Wanted to postpone the trip."

"Why?"

"He said that he can't leave without talking to you."

"Did you talk him into going?"

"I told him that he could also get the jet to bring him back quickly, but going on his quest was important for him."

They arrived at the airport and took the entrance for the smaller aircrafts. Naomi sat up, alert for any sign of Zack. Her mind screamed for her to retreat. What was she trying to prove? Why on earth had she let Brent talk her into this cockamamie idea?

"I brought you to the plane, but this is where you get out and walk to the terminal." Brent playfully pushed her.

"You are irritating. I need the umbrella." She watched Brent run around the car with suitcase in hand. She imagined that he was similar to an annoying big brother.

They huddled under the umbrella and hurried to the terminal. She'd never been in this part of the airport. She'd thought it would be quiet, but it was fairly busy with businessmen and average people.

"What are you doing here? I thought you were gone." Zack spun her around. "You'd left."

"I brought her to you." Brent stepped up between them. "She's ready to go with you to Haiti." To Zack's silence, Brent continued. "Now it's your turn to say the appropriate thing."

"Haiti?" Zack looked at her. Naomi couldn't tell if he was happy or was just confused.

"Um…excuse me, I need to go to the restroom." Naomi headed for the escape route. She'd imagined that Zack would be surprised but thrilled that she'd taken the initiative to join him. Then she let Brent lead her down the fantasy path, and now she felt embarrassed and hurt.

She stood in front of the mirror, examining her face. She splashed the water over her face, blending with the tears that spilled down her cheeks. She doused her face with another handful of cold water, hoping that her eyes wouldn't show any telltale redness.

A knock on the restroom door barely alerted her before the door opened and Zack strolled in. He didn't check the stalls or look around in case any other women were in there. Instead he walked directly to her.

"So Brent told me of his plan to put us together."

"Zack, let's not pretend that we're lovesick teens. What we shared was temporary. We both knew this going in. Although changing the rules midstream seemed like a good idea, it's forcing you to do something that you don't want to do. It's encouraging me to walk away from what I know. Not terribly grown-up, wouldn't you say?"

"Always the logical one." He tilted her chin and waited for her to look into his dark, piercing gaze. "Love doesn't fit in a neat box."

Naomi stepped back. If she didn't allow Zack to touch her, she could keep her thoughts on a rational path. Otherwise, his voice would seduce and turn her into a willing agent for anything he wanted.

"I love you, Naomi."

Naomi blinked. She gritted her teeth to stay firm.

"Not quite the place for my declaration. Circumstances and the time dictate that I not hold back."

A knock sounded on the door. This time Brent's head popped into the doorway. "Guys, not that I'm rushing you, but I've got five angry women ready to beat me down."

"Naomi, I was a fool not to share what I was doing. I knew that going after this information would make others uncomfortable, so I flew solo on the project." He took her hand. "I believed I didn't need you. I was wrong. Do you love me?"

"Yes. I said it before, but you weren't ready."

"I'm a slow learner. Doesn't affect what I know in my heart. I want you to be by my side when I meet my birth mother. I wouldn't share a sacred moment if I wasn't in love with you."

Brent interjected, "Don't play hard to get, Naomi. Security is coming."

"Stop rushing me." Naomi looked into Zack's face. Unlike the moments in the past when he carried his bad-boy image like a proud armor, she saw only raw intensity. His pain was at the surface for the naked eye. She placed her hand over his heart and leaned her head against his chest. She closed her eyes and listened. Her grandmother always said if a woman listened closely, she could hear the true nature of any man.

She looked up in his face. "I love you, Zack. I'd be happy to go to Haiti with you." She hugged him.

He cupped her face. She felt the moisture on her cheeks as her tears made their appearance. He kissed her softly on each side of her face. Then he hovered over her mouth before he kissed her with a soft innocence. "Consider this Part One."

Naomi almost fell over when he stopped kissing her to talk. She craved his touch and could go orgasmic from the touch of his lips on any part of her body. "Part Two had better be worth the wait."

The plane made a smooth entry into the airspace. Naomi offered a prayer of thanks after repeatedly praying for a safe takeoff. The flight attendant didn't shirk her duty with the safety instructions. Naomi listened and looked on with a keen sense of responsibility.

"Relax. Here's a glass of champagne to take the edge off." Zack took the glass from the flight attendant and handed it to her. She took two gulps and emptied the glass.

"Whoa. Pace yourself." He sipped his wine for emphasis.

"It's been a long morning." She defended herself.

"Mr. Keathley, Miss Venable, we have club sandwiches or hot meals for your selection. Since the captain has removed the seat-belt sign, you can move around the plane. The room behind is available if you wish to relax. Simply buzz when you need my services. I'll be in the cockpit, a bit of multitasking."

"I'll skip the meal for the moment," Zack said.

"Me too." Naomi couldn't possibly think about food. Her attention stayed on whether everything was in working order on the plane.

"You are so tense," Zack said when he took her hand. "Come with me."

"Where to?" She hadn't even unbuckled her seat belt.

"Let's go explore the room in the back of the plane."

She was curious. Besides, if she could distract herself on this flight, she was game. She followed him through the door and couldn't help but gasp. "This is unbelievable."

"To say the least."

"What does Brent do again?"

"Besides being an agent, he's had quite the career as a lawyer."

"A successful one, no less." Naomi looked at the double-wide divan that served as a bed. Not only were flowers decorating the room, but a bottle of champagne was in a bucket of ice. The crooning soulful voice of an R&B singer was piped in.

"Shall we enjoy?"

"You don't have to ask me twice." Naomi sat on the divan and reach for a chocolate-covered strawberry.

Within an hour into the flight, Naomi felt herself relax. The champagne helped, but she also appreciated Zack's effort with easy conversation. He'd dimmed the lights, softening their harshness.

She patted the empty spot next to her. Instead of complying, he untied her boots and slipped them off, along with her socks. She wiggled her toes, glad that she'd bothered to get a pedicure.

He slid his hands up from her ankles, along her calves, over her thighs until he reached the opening to her pants. He pulled down the zipper and she gladly wiggled out of the jeans.

The cool air felt good against the heated flush that he created within her. Everything about this day, Zack's declaration, this bumping aircraft, stirred a chord of excitement all sexual in nature that only one man could satisfy.

"Remember I promised you Part Two."

"I hope you don't think that you're done."

"Not by a long shot. I just wanted to direct your attention."

"Enough talking."

"I can do other things with my mouth."

"And tongue."

He chuckled, his lips vibrated against her neck. In one fluid motion, he pulled her T-shirt over her head and laid it on top of her jeans.

"I think modeling agrees with you. That two-piece red number is seriously devilish."

"I didn't know if it would have come in handy for the trip."

"Glad to oblige."

He dipped his finger in the champagne and made a wet trail between her breasts. His finger art consisted of swirls over the cups of the bra sending the nerves into havoc. Her nipples responded as if the bra wasn't in place. She arched up to entice him to use more than his finger to play with her.

Instead he merely kissed the top of each breast with a mere peck. She almost cried out in agony. But still he continued his tease of her body in brutal fashion.

The champagne followed by his tongue made figure eights down the center of her belly. She inhaled when he got to a ticklish spot just above the belly button.

To her discomfort, he poured the champagne directly onto her and then lapped it up. His tongue awakened every nerve under her skin. Every inch of her craved more than his touch.

Her hands ran through his hair and over his face, memorizing the contours before sinking her fingers into the thick muscles of his shoulders.

His lips seared her skin with soft kisses where her panties had covered. Now she couldn't stop from gasping and moaning. Her body writhed as if taken over by an unknown power.

She might as well be under his spell, since his mouth and fingers were like finely tuned instruments that nestled against her and played with her desire.

She craved him with a hunger that seemed deep and primal. As soon as he undressed and donned a condom, she pushed him back onto the divan and mounted him. His hands latched onto her hips for the ride. And she planned to take him on one that he'd never forget.

While they flew tens of thousands of feet in the air, she wanted him to experience floating in a free fall with her. She tightened her thighs and rode him hard and fast, grinding with the need to satiate her hunger.

His guttural cries stimulated her desire even more. She leaned over him looking into the face of the man she loved. The pure beauty of what they had between them stirred the longing in her. Her body and soul were primed.

She quivered her release, controlling and releasing with as much mental strength as emotional. Like an expert dancer, he read her moves in advance and matched her climactic explosion with his.

Chapter 16

Haiti greeted Zack with warm tropical breezes. He felt Naomi's small squeeze on his arm. He touched her hand, grateful for her presence. Maybe by the strength of their love he could make it through this emotional roller-coaster.

They entered the airport, which was a bit subdued, probably due to the lateness of the day, along with the fact that no commercial jets had recently landed.

Zack scanned the scattered crowd looking for anyone who might be waiting for him. Brent had reassured him that everything had been worked out.

"Mr. Keathley?"

Zack nodded and looked at the elderly man whose suit was so crisp that the fabric looked like it held his small frame upright.

"I am Jean Guitard with Blessed Charity. Welcome to Haiti. Welcome home."

In a surprisingly swift move, the man grabbed his face and kissed him on both cheeks. Then he offered Naomi a similar greeting. While Zack remained surprised, she provided a chuckle.

"This is Naomi Venable. She will be joining me."

"I'm sure you're ready to get started, but since it's so late in the day, I think it best to take you to your hotel. Some of the senior staff of the Blessed Charity would like to have dinner with you this evening." He paused. Zack offered a brief nod. "Then in the morning, we'll get started early. I will bring you to the place that was your home for five years."

Zack listened. All the details were nice to know, but he wanted to hear the most important detail. When would he get to meet his birth mother?

"We've sent a letter on your behalf inviting your birth mother to meet you."

"Yes?"

The old man shook his head. "As of yet, she has not responded."

"Oh." Zack turned to Naomi.

"Doesn't mean that she won't come," Naomi said quickly.

"Of course. Miss Venable is absolutely correct. I'm sure she is shocked."

"She knows that I'm here?"

"We told her that you were coming. We only knew of your exact arrival date a couple days ago. We provided an update to her." The man raised his wizen hands in appeal. "You must be patient."

Zack didn't know how to be patient. Besides, did patience mean to wait a few hours, a day, a week? After all this time of wondering and now knowing, he wanted a conclusion.

"I see the concern in your face. We will help in whatever way we can."

He sighed. "I understand, thank you, Mr. Guitard."

"Call me Jean." He clapped his hands together. "Let's head to the hotel."

As they followed the man out of the airport to the parking lot, Naomi leaned closer to him. He looked into her eyes.

"It'll work out," she mouthed.

He nodded, but couldn't muster the confident smile. His stomach churned with the agonizing doubts.

The ride out from Port-au-Prince was like an obstacle course as the vehicles and pedestrians moved as one. Despite the bleak conditions interwoven in the landscape, the children waved at their car.

"We have about an hour's ride into the country-side."

"We'll just sit back and enjoy the beautiful terrain." Naomi patted his knee. "You know, you should really try to live every second of this experience. You can only control what you've been able to get so far. The rest will happen if it's meant to be."

"Oh, no, you've taken the Reba-Frannie pill, now sounding philosophical and darn right."

"Our women tend to do that to us." Jean laughed.

Their trek into the country turned into a bumpy ride with lots of sound effects emanating from the car. Zack wondered if he'd have to push the compact vehicle to the final destination when a strange cough and sputter took over the engine. They shimmied up a steep incline. Just when he thought they were going to have to solicit help from the bystanders, who found the situation humorous, they reached the peak and then coasted for the descent.

Naomi's reassuring pat on his knee turned into a white-knuckle hold for dear life to his thigh. Her nails dug in as they jostled from side to side in the little car.

"We're almost there," Jean called out. His entire being radiated calm.

"Thank goodness," Zack offered. He willed his stomach to stay firm and not force them to pull to the side of the road.

True to his word, Jean entered a village made up of a few buildings and homes scattered over the mountainside. Again, kids emerged full of curiosity.

The hotel looked more like a bed-and-breakfast as they entered. From the outside the building had an understated quality with nondescript color and style. All the energy had gone to decorating the interior. Zack felt the tension ease down his shoulders under the ceiling fans that stirred the tropical breeze.

"Welcome to St. Tropez Guest House. I'm Melinda Johnson. U.S.-bred, but a Haiti convert." A tanned woman with shockingly red hair curled as tight as a poodle's stood in front of them. She was dressed in the local cotton fabric and woven sandals.

Zack introduced himself and then Naomi.

"Now that you will be taken care of, I will leave. But we'll be back this evening for dinner." Jean shook their hands and left.

"Let me show you to your room."

"Oh, we have one room?"

"Yes. Your assistant told me that you needed one room. Was there a mistake?"

"What assistant?" Zack didn't have his personal assistant work on any part of his personal business.

"Brent, lovely man. He is a real charmer."

"Yes, he is." Naomi's laughter rang out.

She showed them to their room. A bare-bones furnished room with bed, desk and chair, and chest of drawers. Although the room wouldn't win awards for interior decorating, it was clean and fresh.

"Breakfast is from eight to nine-thirty. There is also afternoon tea at three. My room is on the first floor. If you need anything, don't hesitate."

Zack nodded. He hoped that his stay wouldn't have to extend to an unbearably long time.

"May I ask what brought you here? We usually get lots of eco-tourists. We also get couples who are interested in adopting." She looked expectantly at them.

"Oh, no. We are here on business." Naomi smiled.

"Well, that's the other possibility." Melinda seemed disappointed that Naomi hadn't clarified.

Zack figured the news of their arrival would have made its way through the village. Chances were probably great that a fantastic story would be created. Maybe they would be mistaken for Hollywood celebrities seeking a baby.

"Is it okay to walk around?"

"Oh, yes. Use the same street savvy that you'd use in the States. People tend to forget common sense when they visit here because of the small-town feel."

"I have Naomi as my protector. I just have to run faster than her."

Melinda threw back her head and screeched a raucous laugh.

Naomi stood on the porch and took the time to study the lay of the land until Zack joined her. She knew of the dismal statistics in Haiti's history, but nothing could diminish the rich culture. Although she felt far removed from the bustling capital, the little village seemed to have its fair share of commerce.

"What are you looking at?" Zack wrapped his arm around her waist and kissed her neck.

"I want to visit the market. I'm sure there's a wonderful assortment of fruit."

"Let's go, then."

The marketplace served as the common meeting place for the exchange of news and selling a variety of items. Naomi liked walking through the stalls, haggling with the vendors for the bargain, listening to the latest news. Some people spoke English or French, but the majority spoke in a patois, a language that her high school French couldn't come close to being of help with.

"We can't carry all this stuff back with us. Customs will not allow you to bring produce." Zack carried the two bags of fruits.

"Stop complaining. We're going to have a wonderful fruit salad."

"We are?"

"Oh, look." Naomi pointed to another vendor. "They've got handmade flip-flops."

"I sense a shopping spree," he said.

"Oh, hush." Naomi had to admit that she was buying more than necessary. But they had managed to not sit around moping over the fact that Zack's birth mother hadn't responded.

Hours passed touring the island's stores. "My feet are killing me." Zack grumbled as the number of bags he held increased.

"Okay. Your whining is killing the buzz. Anyway, we have to get ready for dinner."

"I should have been taking a nap."

"How can you sleep at a time like this?" Naomi said

excitedly. "There's so much to see and do. It's your birth home. Do you feel any connection?"

"No."

Naomi heard the stubborn closure in his tone. His mood was turning and the frustration started to take hold.

She grabbed his mouth and puckered his lips, before planting a sloppy kiss. "Remember, I love you. I'm here with you, no matter the outcome."

He nodded and gave her a small peck.

A few giggles and heckling interrupted their public moment. Naomi smiled, but hurried on her way.

"Oh, so now you want to leave."

"Just bring the bags, Zack." She bit her lip to keep from smiling.

Naomi waited for Zack to finish dressing. He'd grown pensive despite her attempt to keep the mood lighthearted. She suspected that he probably wanted to skip the dinner and wait until tomorrow to see the outcome.

"Why are we meeting these people? This is Brent's handiwork."

"Actually, I think it makes sense. The orphanage is helping you meet your birth mother. Not only did they take you in, but they are also helping in the journey for you to get the healing that you want."

"But I don't need dinner. We could talk, get it over with and let tomorrow come."

Naomi slid off the bed and knelt in front of him. She wanted to see his eyes, into his soul. She wanted to eradicate the fear that grew with every minute that they sat in the room. She placed her hand over his heart, then took his hand and placed it over hers.

"Listen to me."

"Yeah."

"I'm going to be blunt," Naomi prepared. "Your birth mother coming into your life doesn't make or break you. I know you're looking for holes to be filled, but maybe you should look at it as an extra helping of whipped cream, special sauce, whatever. Meeting her will enhance your life but doesn't take away from it if she chooses not to meet you. When you decided to do this, you did it for you. Not her."

"As much as I say that the end result doesn't matter. It did matter. I had the reunion pictured in my mind to go one way. And only one way. I would be in control. I'd find her and decide if I wanted to meet her. I'd listen to see if there was any regret. Instead, it's still being determined if I'm a gift or a burden."

Naomi rested her forehead against his face. "We'll get through this." She kissed the corner of his mouth. "We, Zack. Not you. We will get through this." She kissed his lips, nudging them apart, coaxing them to let her enter to seal the pact between them.

"Can we make love and skip dinner?" Zack asked, his voice loaded with sexy tension.

"Nope. We are going to dinner. And then when we come back, we are going to make love."

"You want the world, don't you?"

"Only if you're in it." She ravished his mouth with a long kiss. "I'm hungry, so hurry it up." She pushed away from him and then turned her attention to the mirror to repair her lip color.

Zack barely made it through dinner, much less through the night. His tossing and turning couldn't have helped Naomi getting a good night's rest, either. Now that he'd made it through the night, he couldn't wait for the morning to begin. The countdown began for the meeting.

While he did consider meeting his birth mother as being pivotal, he had come to terms with its significance, thanks to Naomi's wisdom.

"I figured you wouldn't want a big breakfast. I had Melinda make a fruit salad with our goodies from yesterday." Naomi presented him with a colorful array of fruits.

He picked a piece of guava and popped the sweet fruit into his mouth. He nodded, appreciating the natural sugary treat on his tongue.

Making fast work of the breakfast, he was already on the porch waiting when Jean showed up.

Now to go see where he spent his early childhood. They pulled up in front of a building that looked like a Spanish monastery. The exterior had a fresh coat of paint in a bright pink hue. The trimmings were in violet and the windows were in stark white. The outrageous color worked in an odd sense, since it didn't make him think of a government-run orphanage.

"Does any of this come back to you?"

"Bits and pieces, but everything was a gray color."

"I don't think it was gray on purpose. We recently got a generous donation and used a portion to upgrade parts of the home." Jean showed them into the building and to the main office.

"I remember feeling that this place was a palace. There was a woman who would tell me stories at bedtime. She'd tell me that I was a prince who had been left behind to do great things."

"We don't get much change in our staff. Can you describe her?"

"That was over twenty years ago. She had a small tuft

of hair that was gray in the front. Her glasses would sit on the edge of her nose. Her skin was flawless. I used to think that maybe she was my mother but couldn't tell me."

"That was Alayne DaCosta. She was a missionary from Portugal who worked in the home. Unfortunately, she died about ten years ago from a long illness. I still miss her."

Zack took a deep breath and exhaled. Life moved on. Maybe that was the lesson—move on.

"Can you take us on a tour?" Naomi asked. She continued to hold his hand as if sending her strength and willpower to continue onward.

The tour didn't last long. The orphanage was not large, considering that the building held not only classrooms, a communal dining room and an industrial-size kitchen, but also space for sleeping rooms, the staff's quarters and a couple of offices.

"I feel as though I should take all the children with me," Zack said.

"Many people have the same reaction. These children could use good homes, but they are also not lacking, because many of the donations are from private philanthropists. All our children go on to college or a trade school."

"Maybe while you meet with your birth mother, I could talk to some of the children?" Naomi turned to Jean.

"How thoughtful of you," Jean replied.

"She's a basketball star. She's got stories that can inspire to reach for the stars."

"That's very impressive."

"Well, I'm an ex-basketball star. I think this trip has helped to solidify what I want to do with my life going forward. I know in my heart that my professional basketball career will be in my past."

Zack admired her fortitude. How had this trip helped him? Right now, he treaded in the deep end, hoping that he could make it to the edge and hang on for dear life.

Chapter 17

Zack sat in the community center that had been pre-
determined to be the neutral zone. Jean hovered nearby
but astutely kept his distance. Naomi had surrounded
herself with several older children. Now, after mentally
preparing and emotionally gearing up for one o'clock in
the afternoon on a Thursday in late October, he sat alone
as his heartbeat thudded against his rib cage.

Maybe he should have brought a book. He'd paced
and even dredged up a few tap-dance moves from classes
that he'd attended in Washington.

The clock overhead clicked past the one o'clock
hour. He saw Jean look at his watch. The old man's
concern had taken the starch out of his frame. Zack
knew better than to dress up in uncomfortable clothing
for the occasion. He wanted to be at ease for this waiting
game.

After the second hour passed with no sign, Jean

approached him. "I think…we can try again tomorrow."

Zack nodded. His throat choked.

When he returned to the orphanage, he could barely
look at Naomi. She stayed with the children a little
longer. Grateful for the space, he stayed on safe subjects
about Blessed Charity with Jean.

"I'll take you back to the hotel whenever you're
ready."

"Thanks, Jean," Naomi said. She'd rejoined him
quietly.

"I'll send another note tonight."

"Don't bother." Zack kept his gaze straight ahead.

"Maybe she didn't get the other notes. She could be
ill."

"You know who it is, right?"

"Yes."

"Then you would have heard if she was ill or not?"

"Probably."

"I will go back once more and then I'll return
home."

Naomi leaned her head on his shoulder. Even she had
run out of advice for him.

Naomi opened her eyes, frowning from the sunlight
pouring into the room. "Are you getting out of bed?"

"Soon."

Naomi heard the bad temper in the single word. She
prayed that today would have better results. Her heart
broke for Zack's disappointment. She got up to take her
shower.

"You packed." They hadn't unpacked, but she
noted that his suitcase contained everything, including
toiletries.

"We're leaving this afternoon."

"Oh." So this was it. One final showdown before he left Haiti. The chances of him returning were slim.

After she showered and dressed, he did the same. Another bowl of fruit salad served as breakfast before they headed to the orphanage. This time there were no planned activities to hold their attention until the one o'clock hour.

Naomi spent the time talking to the other children she hadn't met yesterday. She kept an eye on the time and, when he came into view, on Zack.

"It's time," Jean prompted.

"I want you with me this time," Zack said to Naomi.

"Sure. I'm glad that you're stepping up to meet your birth mother. I think it's time that I be the bigger person to reach out to mine."

"I'm here when you're ready to do so."

Together they waited in the community center. Naomi couldn't stop touching Zack to reassure him. She tried to stay neutral, but seeing him in agony revved up her desire to protect him. Now that it was 2:30, she wanted the name and address of his birth mother. She was willing to shake it out of Jean if necessary.

"Let's get out of here," Zack declared with a tone that defied refusal.

Jean nodded.

As they headed toward the door, it opened. Zack halted on the spot. He looked expectantly at the door. A young man stepped into the room. He looked at each one of them before he seemingly gathered his nerve.

"Is Zack Keathley here?"

"That's me."

Naomi felt weak in the knees, much less how Zack must feel.

"I'm Andre Laudat." The young man cleared his throat. "I believe that we share the same mother."

"Is she here?"

Andre nodded. He walked to the door and pushed it open. Then he nodded before pushing it wider.

A woman walked in and stood at the boy's side. She held his arm for support. Her eyes lit on Zack's with fierce curiosity. Her gaze traveled down his body, sometimes restarting from a certain point to travel down.

Naomi couldn't complain. She found herself doing the same to the slender and fashionable woman. The long silence as each side contemplated the other got to her. She strode to the middle and held out her hand. "I'm Zack's friend, Naomi. Pleased to meet you."

The woman had to break her grasp of her son to shake hands. "I'm Lena Laudat." Her voice had a lilting quality, very cultured. Naomi noticed that her hands were delicately soft and manicured. She'd expected a poor girl who had fallen on bad times. The woman who stood in front of her was well-dressed, definitely in a high-end label. Her features were contoured, delicate. Zack bore some resemblance around the nose and mouth, but the strong shape of his face and those dark intense eyes weren't reflected in this woman.

"This is Zack." Naomi felt like the magician or his assistant unveiling sudden appearance of a work of art.

"Sounds very American."

"Actually, it's Azacchus."

"We named him that. His adopted parents kept the

name, which is how the nicknamed developed." Jean, the vigilant host, explained. "Let's all have a seat."

Naomi hadn't decided what to make of Lena. There was nothing not to like. But the words *warm* and *fuzzy* didn't come to mind. She tried not to make comparisons between this woman and Frannie.

"I'd like to speak to Zack alone."

"Yes, of course." Jean hopped up and left the room, followed by the other son.

Naomi hurried after them.

"Naomi will not be leaving."

Naomi motioned to Zack behind Lena's back that he should talk to her.

"No. I don't have any secrets from you."

She tiptoed back to his side. She was wary but pleased to be privy to a very private moment.

"Then she must be very special to you."

"Yes. One day, she will be my wife."

"Ahh…love."

While Lena went on a tangent about falling in love, Naomi tried to stay focused. Did she just get a proposal? She looked at Zack.

"Before I reconnect the dots in my life, I need to know, will you marry me?"

Naomi grinned. "Yes, I will." She turned to Lena, who had tears in her eyes. She didn't want to wait for permission. Instead she hugged the woman tightly.

Her hug wasn't immediately returned, but she felt the arms tentatively go around her. Then the woman sobbed into her neck. She held her there until she quieted.

Zack held a tissue between them. Naomi offered it to his birth mother.

"He means the world to me," Naomi told the older woman as she returned to Zack. He took her hand.

"I often wondered about him. I knew he'd been adopted and I resigned myself into letting fate have control. I was twenty and unmarried when I was pregnant. Many women helped raise him until I had to leave to find work. It was only to be temporary. Unfortunately, year after year passed. I ended up working for a young doctor practicing here as part of his scholarship. We fell in love. He's the father of my five other children—your half-brothers and half-sisters."

"Did you tell them about me?" Zack asked softly, as if afraid of the answer.

"My husband knew and my eldest just learned the truth when the first letter came to me. I had to tell him because I almost passed out when I read the news."

"Did you ever want to find me?"

"Of course. Nothing can erase you from my heart," she said with a sob in her voice. "I knew once I turned you over to the orphanage that I couldn't come back and pop into your life. I didn't want to ruin anyone's life. So I stayed away. I closed the door on the memories."

Naomi removed herself from Zack's hand. She was there for him. She provided strength when he needed it. But now it was time for him to go the rest of the way on his own.

"I'll join Jean and Andre. Both of you need to talk and heal." She hugged Lena and then hugged Zack. "I'll always have your back," she whispered in his ear. "We're our own team now, a force to be reckoned with."

"And I will never let you go. You are my world."

They sealed their pact with a gentle kiss.

* * * * *

L♥VE IN THE LIMELIGHT
Fantasy, Fame and Fortune...Hollywood-Style!

Book #1
By *New York Times* and *USA TODAY*
Bestselling Author Brenda Jackson

STAR OF HIS HEART
August 2010

Book #2
By A.C. Arthur

SING YOUR PLEASURE
September 2010

Book #3
By Ann Christopher

SEDUCED ON THE RED CARPET
October 2010

Book #4
By *Essence* Bestselling Author Adrianne Byrd

LOVERS PREMIERE
November 2010

Set in Hollywood's entertainment industry,
two unstoppable sisters and their two friends
find romance, glamour and dreams-come-true.

KIMANI™
ROMANCE

www.kimanipress.com
www.myspace.com/kimanipress

KPLITLSP

REQUEST YOUR FREE BOOKS!

2 FREE NOVELS
PLUS 2 FREE GIFTS!

KIMANI
ROMANCE ™

Love's ultimate destination!

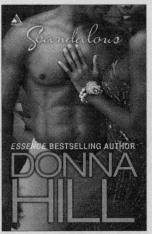